BREAK

GENEVIEVE RAAS

Ravenwell Press

Ravenwell Press

Paperback ISBN: 978-1-944912-15-4
eBook ISBN: 978-1-944912-14-7

First Edition

CHAPTER ONE

Break:

Noun: A weakness in wool, generally uniform through the fleece.

Verb: To smash, split, or divide into parts violently; reduce to pieces or fragments.

BRIAR ROSE

A THOUSAND YEARS BEFORE THE INFAMOUS
EVENTS OF STRAW SPINNING INTO GOLD

D*on't touch the spindle!*
A voice echoed within my ears, pleading and begging. But it seemed so very far away, and the pretty hum from the spinning wheel so lovely.

"Don't be shy, child," the woman cooed. "Come closer."

Flax twisted between her slender fingers, the thread whipping around the spindle as the wheel rocked with every turn of her wrist.

A step closer couldn't hurt. Just one, then perhaps another...

The spindle twirled, the point glinting in the torchlight. I knew it wanted me to reach out to it.

Don't touch the spindle!

I stopped, but my eyes didn't leave the wheel, the twisting thread, that sharp tip of silver...

"I mustn't come any closer," I said. Why did I speak such words? It seems such a silly thing to say.

A second woman approached and reached out to me. Golden hair fell in curls to her waist, and her serene face filled me with trust.

"This is your destiny," she said. "All you must do is reach out and touch the spindle."

She glowed with youth, but her eyes appeared withered and

ancient. A smile curved her pink lips. Her hand remained hovering, waiting for my own.

"Destiny," I repeated. I took her hand, her skin soft as silk beneath my touch.

My destiny.

It all seemed clear now.

The other woman spinning at the wheel increased her speed. The spokes vanished in a blur, and its song grew in intensity, fusing with my pulse.

Don't touch the spindle!

The voice drowned within the clear notes of the spinning spokes, the vibrations crashing over me like ocean waves.

"Yes, that's it my darling." The woman lifted my hand towards the spindle. The beautiful spindle. How pretty it looked spinning and twirling and singing. I couldn't understand why it ever caused me fear.

The spindle glimmered. It wanted to know me. I wanted to know it. To become one with its rhythm.

I stretched my arm and pointed my finger. The hum purred louder. There was nothing else but the hum.

The needle slid into my fingertip.

Elation. Completion.

The room shifted beneath my feet, and the spinning wheel rocked and wobbled before splintering into the stonewalls and the Persian rugs. My legs buckled and the women lengthened as the floor neared me.

Soft arms cradled my shoulders and my head. Their blurred faces spoke and their words drifted along with my thoughts.

"Forgive us," they said. "Sacrifices must be made for the greater good."

Darkness overtook me.

TRISTAN

"The portal at the cliffs is how we will get back to Fate's realm in Dream. It is the only way, and will give us our best chance to succeed," Pater said. "In the meantime, we don't want to arouse any suspicion. We want Fate to think we are honoring our deal, not trying to find his weakness and end him. If we are discovered, I shudder to think of the wrath we will incur."

Holding open his map, he dragged his finger from our current position along a thick line of black that snaked through the Eiger Valley, across the Shadow Moors, and ended at the Crispin Sea. Pater tapped at a skull and crossbones at the ocean's edge, large letters warning CLIFFS OF SORROW.

I'd always wanted to see the ocean, but I never imagined it being like this. Our very lives and souls were on the line; one mistake and Fate would know we were fighting to end his game.

We were now actors in a dangerous gambit, performing a role we didn't fully understand. Not being able to formulate a true plan made me nervous, but our grit was all we had. I tried not to think if we failed.

If my years of confinement and reading taught me anything, it was that one did not double cross deities.

I shivered at the thought.

"Won't Fate be wondering why we don't magic ourselves to the portal once we rescue Briar Rose?" I asked, tightening the saddle to my horse.

"*Magic* ourselves?" He pulled his hand down his face. "I've already explained. Magic has limits. One cannot simply appear wherever they please. A place must be envisioned perfectly in the mind, otherwise one risks losing an arm in one continent and a foot in another. Fate knows this, and won't expect anything more. We can be grateful for this small blessing of time."

"Time? We only have a week until the Blood Moon of Phlegethon."

He tightened his lips as he always did when he didn't want to reveal his anxiety.

"It's all we have."

He folded the map and turned to his horse, placing the parchment in his satchel.

I returned to tightening the straps to my own satchels of books and dried meats. We'd already been traveling for two weeks, and it seemed as if there was no end in sight. An endless cycle of camping, riding, hunting, worrying...

Pater, or Rumpelstiltskin as my mother called him, explained Fate's plot. He wanted to end free will, enslave the world in the name of benevolence. To make matters worse, Pater made a deal with this creature. In exchange for my, and my mother's safety, he offered Fate his very soul, and to find the final sister for their new family.

Briar Rose. A true fairy tale princess.

With her and Pater, the thread of destiny could be spun again, and free will would belong wholly to Fate.

I bit my lip, hating the prickle of fear twisting again in my gut.

I started to fiddle with the amulet I still wore around my neck. It gave me a sense of protection and calm, something I needed now more than ever.

Pater turned towards me, and his eyes narrowed on my chain, but his attention switched to Mother as she approached carrying filled wineskins.

My mother. It still seemed such a strange thing to say. But there she was, the woman I believed dead so long resurrected.

Sun flushed cheeks and a bright smile showed a woman full of youth and determination, but her eyes told a different story. Of an older woman who knew pain, and remained haunted by its ghosts.

She didn't seem the only one haunted by something I couldn't figure out.

Pater straightened and squared his shoulders. He clenched his right hand, then splayed it wide. Passing him, she lowered her gaze to her feet. He left to smother the few dying embers of our campfire.

She handed me a wineskin and beamed at me.

"You don't know how long I've wished to be back by your side," she said. "I should have always been there for you..."

She stroked my hair, her smile turning pained. I reached for her hand and squeezed.

She had endured such grief and remained a beacon of strength. She told me of her torment, of her years locked away in Fate's prison. And how Pater saved her.

"I have no blame of you," I said. "What happened wasn't in your control. Fate is the enemy that tore us apart. He killed my father and took you away from me. There is nothing you could have done to prevent it."

I thought my encouragement would help her. Instead, my words only rimmed her eyes in red.

She pulled away from my grasp and wiped her eyes.

"You look so much like your father," she said, her voice cracking. "The same jaw, the same unruly hair." She brushed it out of my vision. "And your eyes. Like emerald." She froze, as if seeing a ghost. I was sure the loss of her husband still pained her.

Questions burned on my tongue about him. My father, King Edward. I wanted to know about my lineage, about the blood that now made me what I was.

The key to Fate's plans.

Before Fate could imprison his two sisters, Clotho and Lachesis placed Rose under a sleeping curse, one that Fate could never break.

Until me. I held the blood necessary from my parents to break the spell and make Fate's wishes come to fruition.

"Can you tell me about my father?" I asked.

She looked off into the distance, as if thinking what to say.

"He was a...resourceful man..."

Pater stood behind me and cleared his throat. Mother seemed to jump back into the present.

"The horses are ready. We need to get going. Rose isn't much farther now." He pulled out a small, silver flask from his coat pocket, twirled open the cap and drank deeply.

She caught his gaze for a heartbeat. She twisted her gown in her hands. I didn't like seeing her in distress.

I rubbed the ring resting against my chest that had given me strength in dire times. It seemed she needed its protection more than I did. The chain was hot against my fingers as I pulled the necklace over my head.

I held it out to her, the ring swaying gently to and fro.

"Take this," I said. "Maybe it will give you comfort."

She smiled, and reached out, pulling it closer to her gaze. Her mouth opened in horror and she let it swing back towards me.

"What's wrong?" I asked.

Pater walked towards us and looked at the ring. He stiffened.

"Where did you get that?" he asked, his voice low. Dangerous.

"You kept it?" she whispered to Pater.

"Of course I kept it," he replied.

He snatched it from me, letting the ring dangle on the chain from his fingers. It glimmered in the sunlight causing it to nearly resemble gold instead of tarnished silver. Mother turned pale.

She looked at me and forced a smile.

"Thank you, Tristan, but I'm afraid I'm still exhausted from my ordeal, and we have a long day of riding ahead of us. Perhaps we can talk more later?"

"Of course."

She mounted her horse and started off at a slow pace. Pater's eyes followed her. He seemed lost again, as he always did when he watched her.

He turned back and faced me. I hated to look at him. He knew what I had done.

"You entered my chambers that night you snuck off, didn't you?" he asked.

I sighed. There was no point hiding the truth.

"I needed an amulet in order to escape your enchantments. You left the door open," I said.

"I told you never to go in there," he growled. "The damage you could have done."

"It's just an old ring."

His eyes flared. It seemed odd to be so upset over something so insignificant. My annoyance grew from his reaction, but we had come too far to fall back into insults and resentment with each other now.

"You promised me no more secrets, yet I feel like you aren't keeping your end of the bargain," I said, keeping my words calm. Civil.

He took a deep breath, as if to quell his own anger.

"Tristan, there are secrets, and then there are private moments. You've not lived enough life to understand."

He curled his fingers around the ring and buried it deep within his inner pocket.

"You never think I can understand," I said.

He pinched the bridge of his nose and sighed.

"We can't focus on our squabbles right now," he said. "We need to only focus on the task at hand. Retrieving Rose, and discovering where Fate hid Clotho and Lachesis. They are our only hope in ending this madness once and for all. If we fail, everything is lost. Time is our enemy now."

My skin prickled at the thought of it all.

It all seemed so easy at first. Get the princess, release Fate's sisters, smite a deity. But everything in between is what made it now feel impossible.

We had to stay vigilant that Fate never discover our true motives for rescuing Rose. Not just honoring the deal Pater made with him, but for the slight chance she might have information about his sisters. They were our only hope of finding an end to the madness.

And if we failed, Mother's soul would be severed, I would be killed, and Pater would become a slave of Fate along with all of humanity.

"And horrors await us if we fail," I added.

He reached out and laid his hand on my shoulder.

"I've made my sacrifice to get us this far, now I need your help to get us the rest of the way. You might think I keep my cards close, but right now, I'm putting all my trust in you."

My heart swelled. I hated how much I craved his approval, and his need of my help.

"I won't let this thing harm another soul," I vowed, mounting my horse.

He smiled, placing his boot in the stirrup of his saddle. He looked out towards Mother in the distance.

"That's a pretty thought."

❧

WE FORDED THE RIVER HAUG, THAT SEPARATED THE NORTHERN kingdoms from those of the South. I twisted the last drop from my wineskin, and my stomach hungered for something more than dried meat or wild berries.

We kept on, through cramped villages and across empty planes of grass. Hours passed, and unease tightened its grip as any sign of life diminished. Grass turned from green to brown, and trees became twisted dead things.

The sensation of emptiness bothered me the most.

"That's magic you feel," Pater said, riding beside me. "Dark magic. Only curses cause such devastation."

"Why would anyone want to cast such a thing?"

"To break all hope," he replied. "When an enemy loses all hope, they are no longer a threat."

We rode on, Mother still at the helm of our little party. She and Pater continued their tense pattern of silence broken only by rare one word questions and answers. At first this behavior confused me, but I shouldn't be surprised. They shared nothing in common. She was a queen, kind and considerate. Pater was disagreeable and complicated.

Though my resentment still pulsed towards him from our past, I told myself to move on, that things changed. He changed. I now rode by his side, we spoke amiably, and I could finally experience the adventure I always craved.

We had to continue picking up the broken pieces of our relationship. And I knew my desire for us to heal was far stronger than my residual anger.

"I didn't think we'd ever be like this again," I told him.

He raised an eyebrow.

"Like what?"

"Speaking without cross words in every sentence."

He chuckled.

"Yes, perhaps there's hope for us after all."

"I'd like that."

I could tell he wanted to say something more, as if his words swelled in his chest. I wondered when, or if, they would come out.

Silence.

He shifted on his saddle.

More silence.

"I...I fear I owe you an apology," he stuttered. "I was afraid back then. Terrified, really. I've lost much in my life, and...I'm sorry for all the protectiveness, but it was for your own safety. Now, you're getting dragged into the very danger I tried to prevent for you."

I'd never heard him speak so openly. In fact, I didn't know him capable of such feeling. I found myself almost lost for words.

"Start sharing with me. Let me in like you used to, like you are now."

He nodded, clearing his throat.

"I'll try."

I thought on his words. What had he lost that caused such pain? There was something more to his tale than Fate's desire to end free will. Something deeper and longer. I doubted Mother even knew the truth.

Another black tree passed by, charred and desolated. I hated the eerie sensation of despair pressing down on us.

I was struck by a question for him. I didn't know why it came, or why I wanted to know. But it boiled inside of me. It frothed and churned, and I knew I should not ask it.

"Have you ever cursed someone?" I blurted.

He gripped his reins, as if nervous from my question.

"What kind of nonsense is this?"

"I was in your private chambers. You had loads of dark artifacts down there."

"So you automatically assume I go around damning neighboring kingdoms that displease me? Curses are a fascination, but aren't my style."

"That's not what I mean. You are a man of power. Men of power usually have enemies. I mean...I can't see you being too merciful if provoked. Has there ever been a person you...destroyed?"

He turned from my gaze, staring firmly ahead.

"I don't discuss the past," he said, his voice low. Definite. "If you want to speak of the future, the door is wide open."

"But..."

"Tristan, Rumpel! You need to see," Mother's voice interrupted.

I kicked my heels into the sides of my horse, and trotted faster up the hill with Pater to where she looked out.

An absolute world of thorns and brambles twisted and bent beneath us. Gnarled vines wove and contorted into a thick jungle, stretching and clawing out to the horizon.

"What is that?"

"*That* is Rose's castle," Pater answered.

"I don't see any castle. Only pain and misery."

Pater chuckled as he dismounted his horse and stepped closer to the slope. Lifting his hands, he held them out over the thorns. He breathed in and closed his eyes, as if willing the brambles to reveal their secrets.

Five seconds passed, then ten...

"There." He pointed to the center, where the spurs and vines reached higher as if consuming one another. The sun even faded into gloom. "I can feel the magic radiating from within. Clever. Clotho and Lachesis knew what they were doing when they hid her. They even made it poetic with the brier patch. It's beautiful magic."

"It's dangerous," Mother said. "Surely there is another way in there."

He raised an eyebrow.

"It's just some overgrown weeds," he replied. "There really isn't anything to worry about. He is the chosen one. The brambles might put up a fight, but they will fall for him eventually."

"He might be killed before eventually."

"I'll be fine, Mother," I said, though looking down at the sharp points waiting to pierce my flesh I wasn't so sure. Between her fear and Pater's nonchalance, my emotions swayed between fear and determination.

"See, even the boy knows not to worry."

Mother didn't look convinced.

"Can we really trust what Fate told us? How does Fate know Tristan is the one that can break the spell?"

He bit his lower lip, as if considering this fear, then shook his head.

"If there is one thing Fate isn't, it's someone who wastes their own time. Tristan will succeed. He must."

Blood raced through my heart at such powerful words. For a heartbeat, I knew I could conquer anything. I turned my gaze back to the thorns, their points sharp as any spear. My confidence quivered.

Mother pressed her lips together, obviously still not thrilled with the idea. She reached out her hand and touched Pater's shoulder. He looked at her fingers, then at her. His cheeks flushed.

"Do all you can to ensure his protection," she said. "Remember, you are still bound to protect him."

He nodded, not breaking eye contact. She retracted her hand and breathed deep, as if forcing herself back to the present.

He waved his hand my body wanted to break. My knees buckled and I fell into the grass, the clang of metal echoing out. I pushed into the earth and lifted myself, fighting against plates of armor that now covered me entirely.

"What's all this for?"

"To protect your skin from getting scratched, or bones crushed from whatever is inside there," he said. "You best get used to the sensation."

Another wave and Pater held a shield in his left hand and a sword in his right. They were beautiful, like out of the books of brave knights I read so often. He handed them to me, and I couldn't help my heart racing as I grasped the sword.

I pointed it out, admiring the balanced weight of the blade and secure grip of the handle.

"You remember what I taught you?" he asked. "You block and then lunge."

My excitement dwindled as I recalled the last time I had to use his advice. Back at that burnt out house, when thieves tried to rob me of my life. I could still feel the slick blood on my fingers, and hot gore sprayed over my face. But it was the thrill of burying my dagger in another man's chest that chilled me.

I swore never again.

"Will this be necessary to use?"

He shrugged.

"I hope not," he replied. "I don't sense any movement in the castle, but that doesn't mean there aren't other enchantments that might protect the princess. Keep aware of your surroundings. Don't think for a moment you are safe until you kiss her."

My knees weakened again.

"Kiss?"

"How else did you expect to wake her up? Throw water on her?" he asked. "That is the only way this spell can be broken. By a kiss from a prince. You. Really Tristan, there are far worse ways to break curses."

I pressed my lips together, nervous for the sensation awaiting them. I'd never kissed anyone before, and the thought of having to do something so intimate with a stranger bothered me. Besides, no one knew what state she was in. She could be a sleeping skeleton for all we knew. I didn't want my first kiss to be with a corpse.

"After she wakes," Pater continued, "you get the hell out of there."

I shook the image of maggots squirming in a woman's eyes out of my mind.

"What if she doesn't want to come?"

He dragged his hand down his face.

"*What if she doesn't want to come?* Tristan, you either throw her over your shoulder, or pull her along. I don't care if she claws at you while you pull her hair. Use that sword as a motivator if you must. No one said you had to be charming, just efficient."

Biting the inside of my mouth, I looked back at the fortress of thorns and quills.

"Fine, but I'm blaming you if she starts to throw curses at me."

His gaze fell back to Mother. Her eyes narrowed as if not approving of the advice he gave me.

"I'm used to a woman's scorn. What's a little more?"

I rolled my shoulders, trying to get used to the confining sensation of the armor.

"Let's get this over with," I said.

Mother came up to me and gave me a reassuring smile, but I could sense the concern behind her eyes. She pulled me into her arms.

"Be brave," she whispered in my ear. "There's nothing you can't accomplish. I believe in you."

I pulled away, smiling.

Pater remained standing back. I knew I shouldn't have expected any last minute words of reassurance from him.

I took one step towards the brier when a hand clapped my shoulder. I turned to Pater standing right behind me.

"It's a rare moment when I cannot do what is necessary. I want you to know you have my trust in this," he said.

My blood rushed having his faith. That he relied on me. Of course, he didn't have much choice in the matter. Regardless, I appreciated him acknowledging my use all the same.

Guilt came with it.

"I didn't mean to upset you earlier, or to push you to share your past," I said.

"I...I was a different man then."

"I know."

"Then let's stay here in the present, and win our future. Together." A type of sincerity bled from him asking me to believe in him. To trust him.

He put out his hand to me, waiting for my own.

I paused, thinking of his words. Of his earnestness.

I grasped his hand, and gave it a firm shake. I wanted his trust just as much as he wanted mine.

He stepped back, and I walked towards the thick hedge of spines and thorns, not knowing what I would face, or if I would even succeed.

CHAPTER TWO

The sun faded as I neared the thick jungle of thorns. Gray mist loomed within the branches, and the scent of earth and mildew filled my nose. Warmth didn't exist in this place, only dread.

Standing before the great hedge I gulped. The wall stretched so high I almost lost sight of it. And when I tried to peer inside, I wished I could be anyone else. There weren't only the large spikes I had seen from the hill, but smaller, sharper barbs on every inch of the branches.

I sucked in a breath, forcing myself to press on.

I unsheathed my sword and closed my grip tight around the handle. Lifting it over my head, I brought the blade down with all my force onto the branches. The entire structure groaned and shook, but the blade didn't even scratch through the heavy bark. Instead, the tight patchwork curled tighter together. As if telling me that's not how to play the game.

There was only one way through, and for a heartbeat I was grateful for my armor. At this point, I welcomed anything that acted as a barrier between the sharp pricks and my skin.

I gripped one of the outer vines, thick with age and magic. Weaving my fingers around the spines I pulled, testing the resistance. It gave. Placing my other hand carefully on another branch, I shoved.

One foot in.

The brier quaked, fluttering and shaking around me.

A second foot.

I pulled and shoved and moved and tore.

The sharp thistles scraped against my armor as I squeezed through. My heels sank into the mud. Gnarled vines threatened to trip me with every step. I couldn't lower my guard a second, fearing one wrong move and I would fall and impale myself on a thorn.

Another groan came from the brier. It vibrated into my bones as I squeezed the branches apart, continuing to push forward. Always forward.

The further in I ventured I seemed to enter another section of the brier. The density of the patch lessened, but the thorns grew larger. Sharper. Deadlier. I believed myself walking through a thick forest of spears.

A flash of red caught my eye in the distance. I ducked below branches twisting overhead as I inched closer. A fleck of white. Closer still. A swatch of blue.

I pulled back another vine, and my stomach twisted.

A man, or what was left of a man, hung limp from a thorn, his armor rusted and clothes in tatters. The spike ran him through his chest, the tip stained brown from his blood. His shriveled skin made his teeth protrude and froze his final expression, preserving his fear and agony.

I tried to retreat, but the vines constricted tighter together preventing me. The branches growled. My blood raced hot through my heart.

I continued on, having no choice.

Another dead man. This one dressed in rotting blue and rusting armor, his head lolled back, a thorn impaling him from his groin up through his back.

I wanted to retch.

These were other men who attempted the same feat as I attempted now. I prayed I would be luckier.

I gripped the nearest vine and pulled myself forward, the vines behind me snapped and cracked, knitting together. Chasing me, as if I were a fly in a spider's web. I pressed forward, the branches splitting and creaking, hungering. I knew, though I didn't know how, the time for feeding approached.

It was a living being, and that terrified me above everything else.

Taking out my sword, I tried to break free through the vines, but all my force vibrated back through my body. The brier growled, no, roared!

Branches tore through the gloom and wrapped themselves around my wrists. I tried to kick, but more brambles shot up from the ground and tied my ankles, then my legs, and snaked around my waist.

The more I struggled, the tighter my bonds squeezed. My fingers tingled and I thought my ribs would crack. Spurs and pricks dug into any crevices in my armor.

The brier pressed my back into the ground. My helm flew off my head, and all breath left my body. A ceiling of thorns rippled like waves above me, growing closer.

A single thorn, thick as a tree and longer than two men, lurked towards my head. I pressed back into the dirt, trying to get as much distance as I could. Closer it crept, stopping a breath from my forehead. The vines creaked and moaned. The sharp spine moved down right between my eyes.

I shivered as the cold wood pressed into my hot skin.

Down it scraped, over my nose and down my throat, until it stopped at the soft dip at the base of my neck. My heart pulsed against the spine and the brambles fluttered.

"Are you a contender, or are you my supper?" the brier whispered within my head.

"Con...contender," I pressed out, gasping for air.

The thorns fluttered again, as if laughing.

"That's what they all tell me, Food," it replied. "I must taste."

I struggled again, trying to push it away from my neck.

A sharp bite blazed through me. Pain seared down my veins and into my heart. Heated liquid ran across my neck. Blood, my blood. I clenched at the agony, wishing the thorn would just take me and be done with it.

The ground quaked.

"You," the brier spoke, its voice a mix of disappointment and wonder. "Contender. The blood of the prophesied prince."

The thorn retracted, flying back from wherever it came. The vines around my wrists and ankles fell slack, and I ripped myself away and stood. The brambles curled and bent opening before me, revealing a path of gray stone leading to a door of heavy wood.

I rubbed the base of my neck, checking the depth of the wound. It stung, but it wasn't deep as I feared. My blood had saved me. What Fate had told Pater was true.

This was my destiny.

Picking up my sword, I navigated the path of crumbling stone. I turned the door handle, but large chunks of rusted metal broke apart in my hand. I struck the door with my shoulder, putting all of my strength into it. I found that was hardly necessary, as the door gave no fight, opening easily and letting me spill onto a cold marble floor.

I pushed off the stone and righted myself. Dust and decay surrounded me. This place had not seen life for a millennia. I walked farther in, my footsteps echoing out into the silence that seemed almost sacred. I felt an intruder.

Exploring deeper, I passed through halls painted in fading reds and golds depicting exotic animals and men wearing togas. I kept moving through. Petrified food laid out on a set table, a thick layer of soft dust causing it to appear carved out of stone.

I turned and entered a room to the right, then through more halls of painted rescues and floors of once brightly colored tiles. Marble statues stood in odd places. Some laid across carved chaises, while others were grouped as if in conversation. The detail of these figures astounded me, as I never knew such artistry possible.

Entranced, I approached a woman. Braids and ringlets of hair coiled in fantastic arrangements against her head. Perfectly carved earrings hung from her ears, and the curve of her lips made a pleasant smile. Her toga appeared of finest silk, so real and delicate, I couldn't help but touch it.

The fabric moved. A waves of dust rolled off her gown and arm where I had brushed. Below lay bronze skin.

These weren't statues at all. They were real people, frozen in time as a moment captured forever.

I backed away. Horror gripped me and a cold sweat dripped down my back. Everything in me wanted to run away, but I knew that wasn't possible. I had to find Briar Rose first. Only then could I get out.

I hurried through more halls and rooms. I tried to ignore the people sprinkled throughout, but their petrified faces were haunting. Laughing faces, annoyed faces, faces, faces, faces.

Where was Briar Rose?

My hope started to dwindle, and fear started to take me over.

I tried to think back to the fairy tales I'd read as a child. There was something in common with many of them.

The answer caught my gaze as I looked out a window at a tower.

Of course.

I snaked my way towards the tower door. I didn't even bother with the rusted handle this time. I kicked open the door, the hinges breaking completely. A flight of stairs spiraled up.

I ran up the curving stone steps, my lungs burned as the weight of the armor pulled down on me.

Another one of the stone people, a woman, sat on a chair outside another door, as if guarding whatever lay within. Hope washed over me that this would be the right place.

Opening the door, I expected another room covered in dust. Instead, color, vibrant and pristine color, awakened my senses. While the rest of the palace laid in waste of faded reds and powdered grays, this room was fresh and clean.

I stepped across beautiful mosaics of men and women dancing. The deepest red painted the walls, lions and tigers leaping through a wild scene. None of this grace compared to the woman lying on her back on a bed of purple silk sheets.

A toga of delicate pink covered her sleeping form. The silk cupped her breasts and lay still against her stomach, draping over her hips. I wanted to reach out and stroke her hair of gold.

My heart raced for her, this beauty of ages past preserved. For me alone. An odd thought, I admit, but it excited me. To think how time separated us, but now we would be united at last, all because of a kiss.

My lips tingled. I wanted nothing more than to claim her mouth, to awaken her and bring her back into the world. It was as if a rhythm vibrated out of her, calling to me. Wanting me.

I neared her, taking soft steps.

Serenity made her face glow, and a mixture of lilac and rose brightened her skin. Pink lips were flushed the same shade as her soft cheeks. Had I been told she was an angel, I would have believed it.

I bent down, nearing, staring, worshiping...

A screech sounded behind me. The spell broke.

I turned, horrified, as the woman from outside lunged at me. Hands bent like claws swiped at me, scratching at whatever they could grasp.

I pulled out my sword and pointed it directly at her chest. She didn't care. Dust and dirt sloughed off of her. Her eyes were dead, and skin withered.

I charged her. She reached for my neck. My sword dug into her ribcage. I cringed recalling the same sensation of metal grating against bone. She screeched again and backed away, slipping off my blade.

Terror flooded me. I expected blood to gush from the wound, but none came. What was this thing? I tried to cut her down, but she caught my sword. She wrapped her fingers around the blade. I tried to pull it from her grasp, and my blood turned ice.

The bones cracked in her hands as she strengthened her grip. I tugged hard as I could, wiggling the sword to cut off her fingers. I might have well done nothing. She tore the blade from me, throwing it to the floor. Faster than I could see, she shoved me against a wall. She screeched again, as if inhaling a scream. She might not have been made a stone, but she had the strength of rock.

Her cold, icy fingers dug into my skin. She gripped my jaw and forced my head up, exposing the wound where the thorn had tasted my blood.

"You got past the thorns, the first to do so, but it does not mean you will survive me," she rasped. "My lady will not suffer imposters."

Leaning closer, she pressed her two fingers into the gash. Pain throbbed at the base of my throat.

She removed her hand, my blood bright against the gray still shrouding her skin. Her eyes made me chill as they searched me. Opening her mouth, she sucked my blood clean off her fingers.

Was this my end?

"Your day has come," she wheezed.

She released her grip and I fell to the floor. What would she do with me now? A glint caught my eye. My sword lay right beside me. I turned and reached, bringing it back in front of me. I would not die without a fight.

No one was there.

I stood, searching the room for her, but she had utterly disappeared. I wiped the cold sweat from my brow, the creature's voice still ringing in my ears, *your day has come.*

I recollected myself best I could as I turned back to Briar Rose. I had to kiss her before any more surprises leapt out at me.

Sitting beside her, I leant down without thought or ceremony and touched her lips with mine.

The world fell away with our kiss. Only she and I existed in that space. Soft heat rippled through my body, erasing any residual fear from moments before.

I knew then there would be no other I would ever want to kiss.

She stirred. I broke from her lips and moved back. Her eyelids fluttered and she sucked in a deep breath. Turning her head, she focused on me and gasped.

Worried I frightened her, I put out my hands to let her know I meant no harm.

"Are the sorceresses defeated?" she asked. "Did you vanquish them?"

She rose from her bed and stumbled to the door and looked out.

"I'm afraid I've only accomplished waking you."

"Then it continues," she whispered, dismayed. "How long has it been?"

I hated even telling her.

"A millennia," I replied.

Her gaze grew distant, as if staring through me. She gripped the fabric of her toga into her fists.

"It's all my fault. I knew I shouldn't touch the spindle, but it seemed such a harmless act. It called to me, and I was too weak."

Anger and disappointment filled her words. I took her hand in my own, and held it tight hoping to calm and reassure her. I wanted to hold it forever.

"That doesn't matter now," I said. "The curse is broken, but there is still much work ahead of us. I need your help."

She looked at me, as if noticing me for the first time. Her eyes fell down to my neck, which still stung.

"You're hurt." She took a step towards me, but her legs were obviously weak and she tripped. I caught her and our lips were but a breath apart. I wanted to claim them again, but shook it away. Now was not the time.

"It doesn't matter, we have to get you out of here."

"Leave? But what about my kingdom? I cannot abandon it now if the threat remains."

I remembered what Pater said about throwing her over my shoulder. I could never do that to her.

"If you want to protect your kingdom, then you need to trust me. The sorceresses you speak of survive. We are all entangled in a plot greater than any of us. If we want to vanquish this threat for good, it can only be with your help."

She was about to reply when the room rumbled. Thunder roared down the spiral stairs. I shoved her behind me and held out my sword.

Figures covered in dirt and grime burst in, clouds of dust curling off of their skin. A cacophony of voices filled my ears, the group pushing and squeezing past one another all to get a look at the princess.

Tears streamed down their faces, washing away the gray, revealing fresh skin beneath.

"Silence. Out of my way!" a man bellowed. "Let me pass."

A man pushed through to the front. A crown sat atop his powdered hair, and dulled jewels bedecked his every finger. His gently aged face showed a man of ease, but his eyes showed a man of arrogance.

His mouth opened as he looked the princess up and down.

"It's true!" he exclaimed. "I never thought I'd see you again."

He opened his arms to her and she rushed into them and embraced him. He pulled her in tight.

"Rose, you are awake. Praise the gods!" He pulled back, placing his hand on her forehead and cheeks. "Are you well? Do you have a fever?"

She pulled his hand away and smiled.

"I'm fine, all thanks to this man."

She motioned towards me. Her father's gaze met mine, and I straightened my stance.

"You've returned my daughter to me," he said. "I must know the name of our savior."

"Tristan." I remembered that wasn't quite correct anymore. "Prince Tristan."

His lips pulled into a sincere smile, but somehow it didn't fill me with confidence.

"Prince Tristan, you have my eternal thanks, and my kingdom owes you a great debt."

"If that's the case, I'm afraid I must collect it now."

"Name it. You've returned the life of my daughter, saved our lands, and ended the danger. I will not deny you."

I wasn't even sure how to say it.

"As I was trying to explain to your daughter, the battle is not over yet. If we have any hope of succeeding, I must leave now and take the princess with me."

He stiffened, and his right eye twitched. He looked behind him at the collection of courtiers and servants.

"Leave us," he commanded them. They left, reluctantly, and he turned his attention back to me.

"Don't speak of such nonsense in front of my court," he said. "I don't want them upset. It's obvious the curse is broken. What more danger could there be?"

"Indescribable danger, sir," I replied.

He lowered his brow, and clenched his jaw.

"My family brought together. My kingdom restored. And now you ask to tear it apart within a minute? No, I will not allow that. I cannot. I will not be thrown into more chaos."

"But sire, chaos is already at your door. It never truly left."

He crossed his arms.

"Do you want gold? How about my rings? Take them all, but I will not listen to any more of your babbling."

"Father..." Rose said. "Listen to him. We cannot sit idly by."

He sighed.

"I know you want peace. We all crave it, but it can't happen unless the sorceresses are vanquished," I said.

I knew I didn't tell the entire truth. That Rose was the only way to keep up the sham with Fate, and hopefully her knowledge could give us the edge we desperately needed. That we really weren't wanting to defeat the "sorceresses," but find them to defeat the true enemy.

If I explained this, I knew I would lose them both for sure. Blaming these sorceresses was the only way. I couldn't risk Rose's willingness, and I had to reach the king's reason, if any existed.

"I am preparing to vanquish them once and for all. Peace will be brought back. But for that to happen, I need Rose."

"Why?" he asked. "Why her and not someone else?"

"Because she's always been the key. It's why she was targeted," I said. "Sire, my mother was also cursed by this same evil. They destroyed my family. They killed my father. They took my kingdom, too. Now we have a chance to restore everything to its former glory."

He thought. Then he thought more.

"No," he replied. "I can't let you take her now I have her back. Look at us, we are pitiful creatures lost to time. How long has it even been?"

I found I couldn't answer him, fearing his response.

"A thousand years," Rose said.

His features sunk to despair, then hardened in his resoluteness.

"My gods," he breathed. "This is why you will not have her. I've waited long enough to get my life back. I am done chasing monsters, I'm done fighting wars that cannot be won. The only way to move forward is to stop chasing danger that only damns us further."

I didn't want to admit he had a point, in a small way. But it became clear to me he wasn't only arrogant, but a coward. And his cowardice would be the end of Rose again, as it clearly had been a millennia ago. But he wouldn't see that, he wouldn't accept the blame.

The thought sent a chill down my spine.

"Father, this thing still breathes. It still hungers for us. I beg you let me go. I want to go."

I loved her bravery. Her father held out his hand, silencing her.

"Enough. I will hear no more of it."

He clapped his hands, clouds of dust rolling into the air. A servant rushed up the stairs.

"While some people want to fret over nothing, I think we should celebrate victory. Celebrate life. Prepare what food you can. Tell the courtiers to wash themselves. We will hold court once more. We will take back what life we can salvage."

The servant blinked, then cleared his throat, obviously nervous at the news he had to tell.

"Sire, there is no food. In fact, there isn't anything but shattered clay pots and tarnished spoons. Our clothes are in tatters and whispers abound that we will not last. The palace is crumbling to pieces. It's unsafe."

"Unsafe!" The king took in a breath, as if trying to quell his rage at the truth he insisted on denying. "Gather what you can. The men will go out and hunt, while the women collect water from the river to clean the muck off our skin. We will make camp in the courtyard. As we've been reduced to animals, we might as well live like them."

The servant nodded and ran out.

"So you are going to bury your head in the sand? Live outdoors?" I asked.

"Until we can rebuild, yes. Sacrifices must be made to keep the kingdom together and moral high. Once we have food in our bellies things will look better. We cannot be separated."

He was lost to delusion. Or worse, fear.

"How will the moral look when the sorceresses return? It's not a matter of if, but when."

"I agree with the prince," Rose said. "It's not right to hide. To pretend. This thing needs to be faced once and for all. It's the only way to truly be together, to regain our life."

He shook his head.

"I know you both see a coward before you, but you have bravery confused with suicide."

I could see I fought a losing battle. I believed Rose felt the same. She seemed willing to go with me, and I considered taking her myself. But I knew her father would fight, and I didn't want to harm him. Even if we did get past him, the court and soldiers waiting below would insure we didn't get far.

I was running out of options. I wished Pater was here. He was the superior negotiator, which I hated admitting.

"Come now," he said. "Stop looking so cross at me, Rose. Please, focus on celebrating the victory of your resurrection. We will rebuild the kingdom, although it might take a little time."

It struck me how I might get through to him.

"I understand now I asked too much in separating a father from his daughter." Rose shot me a confused look that bordered on anger. "And

I hate that you are reduced to such squalor, especially on a joyous day like this one."

"What I would give to have a feast like we did before those sorceresses threatened us. Before they succeeded in their curse. To have our home a home, and not rubble. It would make it so much easier to forget the nightmare," he said.

"I know who can solve your predicament."

CHAPTER THREE

Cards:

Noun: An instrument or machine for carding fibers that consists usually of bent wire teeth set closely in rows in a thick piece of leather fastened to a back

Noun: An issue especially with emotional appeal that is brought into play to achieve a desired end

RUMPELSTILTSKIN

I **stared out** over the brier of thorns and brambles hating being utterly useless.

Not many instances passed in my life where I couldn't be in control. Plans were always my strength. Assurance where I thrived. Now, in the battle that mattered most, I could only grasp at straws.

I had to depend on a boy with no experience. I had to gamble we would find Fate's weakness, if one even existed. Worst of all, I had to rely on hope, a sentiment I was not used to enduring. I didn't like the sensation. In fact, it terrified me.

Hope is uncertain.

I tapped my fingers against my leg as I watched and waited. Minutes turned to hours, time laughing at me as it slipped past.

We only had until the blood moon. Seven days. I prayed the girl would be of use, that her memories might reveal some clue, some snippet of information that would lead us to Fate's sisters, and that they would lead us to his end.

Briar Rose was the last to see Clotho and Lachesis free, after all. She had to know something.

If she didn't...

I didn't like that thought. I didn't like what it meant.

Within you lies the key, the Oracle had once told me. *Allow it to guide your way.*

I shoved the Oracle's voice out of my head, hating the chill radiating down my spine. It hadn't come to that yet.

I paced back and forth, my mind reeling wanting to know every second of what transpired away from my gaze.

"It's been hours. Do you think he is ok?" Laila asked, her voice shaking me back to the present.

"Yes," I replied, though I didn't know. I didn't want her to worry.

I didn't know why I still cared.

She returned to her books and diagrams, her eyes scanning pages filled with myths and monsters. She told me books were invaluable resources for hidden information that might prove useful. While I agreed, I favored a more hands on approach.

Her mouth opened slightly, and she gently mouthed the words she read. She wet her lips and I thought I would be undone.

I took out my flask and took a swig of whiskey. It burned delightfully down my throat and within my veins. I needed something to numb the sensations in my chest, and the memory of her lips on my own.

I sat down in the grass, my back to her. The crinkling and flipping of parchment from her book filled my ears. As did her breaths...

I took another drink. Heat flooded my veins, and loosened my tongue.

"I'm sure Tristan will have those happy thoughts of his father you poisoned his mind with to get him through the brier patch," I said, though it came out more like a growl.

The grass rustled beneath her, and I knew she must have turned towards me.

"It is a great burden knowing a father is horrid," she said. "I know from experience, if you don't remember. I rather him believe a lie than know the truth. The truth is too painful."

"You mean the truth of us?" I was surprised by the bitterness in my words.

"I never said it was about us."

I twisted and faced her.

"You don't have to." I let out a slow breath, calming myself. "We agreed Tristan must never be told the truth of what happened between us, but letting him believe his father a saint is grotesque."

"It might be grotesque, but so are we."

She turned back away and paged through her book again. I returned to staring out at the brambles, the haze of everything between us remaining thick and heavy.

I kept trying to convince myself I didn't need her love, but I knew it was a lie. Since she told me we never could be, that my love was disgusting to her, I yearned for my once hardened heart. But what good had it served me even in the past? Since the first time I saw her, she cut through it and split me to my core.

And no matter how much I bled for her, she wouldn't be swayed in her resolve. Not even when I offered Fate my very soul in exchange for her own.

I opened my palm, the gnarled scar from Fate's scissor's pulling and stretching. A reminder of our deal. I didn't tell Laila how the scar deepened with every passing day. I especially didn't tell her of the sensation of being tethered to something other than myself.

Splitting and cracking carried on the wind. Laila and I stood. The ground vibrated beneath my feet, and the entire brier patch rumbled filling my ears with thunder.

Thorns shriveled. Brambles disintegrated. Vines twisted in agony as they split and snapped. The once impassible brier crumbled to the ground, revealing a palace of mildewed stone in the center.

My heart leapt in my chest. Tristan succeeded.

But the rusted gates remained closed, and I held my breath begging for Tristan to emerge with Briar Rose.

"Where is he?" Laila asked.

I couldn't answer. The brier remained thick and dangerous, and the magic strong. Blood ran cold through my veins, and my shoulders tensed with waiting.

Still, no one.

A low grinding sound came from the castle, of disintegrating metal straining through old gears. The gate slowly opened.

I sucked in a breath, not even realizing I ever stopped. We could finally start our race towards our salvation, or damnation.

My hopes were dashed as two men rode out on horses towards us, neither one Tristan.

I pushed Laila behind me as they approached us, trying to ignore her hot skin beneath my touch. The horses whinnied and blew rolls of dust from their flaring nostrils. White powder creased in the men's brows and around their noses.

"Are you the great sorcerer?" the one on the left asked, his chest smeared with dirt and sweat.

"That depends," I replied.

"Prince Tristan has told our king of your skill. His majesty wishes you at court immediately, along with Queen Laila," the other said.

Damn Tristan and his big mouth, telling things that ought not to be told.

"What is this about?" I asked.

"We do not question our king, only obey his command."

The horses struck the ground, as if feeling their master's impatience with me. Something about this made my skin crawl. I didn't trust kings, and I didn't like agreeing to terms I didn't know.

"He is not my king, and I do not have to obey," I spat.

Their eyes narrowed, and their grips tightened on the reigns.

"But Tristan is your prince, no?"

I ground my teeth.

"Technically," I responded.

"And you do not obey your prince?"

"This is ridiculous!" Laila cut in. "Take us to my son."

She moved towards her horse, placing her foot in the stirrup. I grasped her wrist, stopping her. Her gaze met mine, and I swallowed hard.

"I don't like this. We don't have the time," I whispered.

"Because arguing saves so much time." She rolled her eyes. "If you haven't noticed, we don't have much choice. If you want to stay and play a game of wits, be my guest. I'm going."

She hoisted herself up on her horse then dug her heels into the animal's sides, riding off.

I clenched my jaw. That woman could be insufferable at times. Most times.

"Well?" the other man asked.

I mounted my horse, cursing.

Everything in me told me it was a mistake to go. But what choice did I have?

THE MEN HEAVED AND GRUNTED AS THEY STRUGGLED TO OPEN A SET of petrified wooden doors.

Idiots.

I flicked my wrist and the entire door of stone disappeared. Their eyes widened and their mouths dropped. I can't deny my enjoyment at their shocked faces.

I still loved watching mortals squirm when I displayed the simplest of spells. Besides, I wasn't going to let their incompetence stand in the way of losing precious seconds.

Laila's gown swept the floor, causing rolls of dust in her wake. The mosaics crumbled beneath my leather boots, and I hated passing beneath ceilings that threatened to collapse if one breathed too hard.

The men kept a quick pace as we passed beneath crumbling arches and into rooms of dimly lit candles. It smelled of must, mold, and residue of cardamom. Birds flew in front of us, entire walls collapsed allowing nature inside.

Finally, we entered a chamber filled with people. At least, I believed them to be people.

Swathes of silk and cotton flopped over their shoulders and hung down passed their hips to their sandaled feet. But the dust covering them made my breath stick in my throat. Some wiped away what grime they could from their faces, smears of dirt and decayed makeup causing them to resemble monstrous creatures.

They were relics of a time long passed.

Only two stood out from the white and gray. Tristan and a young woman, who had to be Briar Rose. She had a simple beauty about her, though her forehead was a tad large and her nose too slender. She was a waif, and I feared any hardship we faced on our journey might break her.

Tristan stood at her side, his eyes riddled with anxiety and soul blazing with despair. I could always sense a desperate soul, peer into its fears and desires. It's what gave me that razor edge in the deals I made.

His burned so earnestly.

I immediately knew everything he wanted to tell me in that first, sweet rush. How he feared losing Rose's trust, how he couldn't harm her father, how he didn't know what to do. The boy always worried too much about other people's feelings, and as usual, it was up to me to save the day and do what needed to be done.

"I'm told you can assist me," a dry voice said.

It came from a man sitting on a disintegrating throne, a tarnished crown sitting atop his dirty hair. His face was gaunt, and cheeks sunken. He seemed a man few would question if they enjoyed keeping their head.

"To what do I owe this pleasure?" I asked. I let my irritation slip through.

His eyes flashed. He leaned forward, gripping the ends of his arm rests.

"Do you not bow before a king?" he growled.

I raised my eyebrow and looked around, before setting my gaze back to his.

"I do believe that to be a king, one must have a kingdom. You clearly have only rubble."

His knuckles turned white as he dug his nails harder into his chair from my truth. A small flame sparked within his soul. Pain. Sorrow. Misery. It smoldered and fermented, awakening a hunger within me for it.

I'd consumed countless despondent souls, their anguish feeding my need for more. It was a kind of curse, really. To always be hungry, but never fully slaked.

But his, his was different. I'd never devoured the soul of one so ancient. Curiosity as to its purity and sensation throbbed deep in my gut. What beautiful torment would I taste?

"I will ignore your insolence," he said. "For the very fact that it is true. I don't have a kingdom anymore. We were once powerful, a force in the world. Now, we are reduced to live like animals in squalor."

"How does this affect me?"

"I want you to restore it. Bring us back to our former glory. I want my life to return to how it was before this nightmare. I want my court to be dripping with gold and jewels and bellies filled with wild boar."

"Seems relatively straight forward."

"You can do this thing, then?"

"I can."

The king clapped his hands, a smile stretching from ear to ear. "Wonderful!"

"Just wait, you never asked me the more important question."

His smile sunk.

"Which is?"

I chuckled.

"'Will I?'"

"Well, will you?"

"That depends on what I'm offered. You have no wealth, no land. You have nothing, in fact. That's not much of an incentive."

He tapped his fingers against his chair, and his eye started to twitch.

"I'm sure an arrangement can be met. Name your price."

I shot my gaze to Tristan, sensing the problem once more, how Rose and her Father blamed Clotho and Lachesis for their curse. The sorceresses.

"I believe you already know the price. The accompaniment of your daughter, Rose."

The king stood, and stepped towards me.

"Prince Tristan told me you would be of service to us," he said. "Not that you would try to steal my daughter from me as well!"

"You damn your kingdom and your daughter for good if you don't take my deal," I said. "I'm offering you a way to make sure you remain safeguarded forever. Not that I patch an immense crack in a foundation with sand."

His face reddened with anger.

"You dare tell me I want to damn my own daughter? I want nothing more than her safety."

"Then prove it," I replied. "Right now you are a broken man believing life can go back to warm summer nights and honied wine. Such desires are dangerous when the thing that destroyed your life remains."

He shook his head.

"I don't believe you. How could the sorceresses still care about us after a millennia? Tell me. They are satisfied with the punishment and will not bother us again."

"What is a millennia to such creatures?" I asked. "A blink. Trust me, they will return, and they will be out for blood this time. If you want your kingdom restored as you say, if you want Rose safe, then she must come with us. Your daughter is the key to their defeat."

His flame of despair burned brighter now. So bright. I wanted to touch it.

"I won't let you take her."

"Father," Rose said, stepping to him. "You didn't listen to the warnings the last time, and look what happened. Heed what he says. We can't pretend the threat is gone."

Smart girl. I was glad at least one of them had some sense.

"You should listen to your daughter," I said.

He faced her, shaking his head.

"If this man thinks he is going to rip you away from me after getting you back, then he will pay," he spat.

I stepped closer to them, my shoulders square and stance definite. He slowly turned his face to mine.

His flame quivered with fear. With want. With need of what I could give him. Deep down, in a place he would deny existed, he wanted what I promised.

"Just take what I offer," I said.

He snapped his fingers, and guards rushed me pointing their rusted swords at my chest. I laughed.

One twist of my wrist and they flung against the walls. I preferred to break their necks, but I knew murder was not a good first impression for the princess, especially if I wanted her confidence.

The king ran up back to his throne, pulling Rose with him. She tried to pull out of his grasp. Tristan jumped to her, but she waved him to keep his distance.

"Again, I am threatened by magic," he said.

"Not threatened," I cooed. "Given an opportunity."

He moved Rose behind his back as I approached, taking each step slow. I felt like a cat on the prowl.

"I won't have her be put in unnecessary danger," he snapped.

I sighed.

"You are making too big a deal about this," I said, making sure my voice was calm and smooth as honey. "It's quite simple. You want your kingdom restored, and I can make it so."

His flame blazed. I stood right before him, and reached out my hand laying it over his heart. Heat flooded me, a strong yearning for the want within him.

"Remember your life before the horrors and threats began? Think of those days in the sun beneath your vineyard. You yearn for them. For peace. I can bring those days back again. I can give you a life of happiness and safety. Your kingdom will be powerful, and your daughter the heir to a great empire. This is yours in a second, all it takes is for you to say 'yes'."

Sentiment poured from him. He absolutely reeked of it. I smiled. Sentiment was weakness.

His eyes softened, and his shoulders relaxed as he looked at me.

"I've missed those days," he said, as if he were five years old again.

"I know," I cooed.

I sensed him wavering, suffering, wanting more. My pretty words tempted him. They always did.

"The price is too great, too..." he whispered.

"Shush," I said. "With me, you have certainty of joy and happiness. If you refuse, you are left with certainty of death and your daughter lost forever. Do you really want to make that mistake again?"

"Father, take what he offers!" Rose pleaded. Her cheeks were red with frustration.

I twisted my wrist and a scroll of parchment and quill appeared in my hand. I held it out to him. He looked, and he thought.

"No," his voice cracked. He pulled away, breaking free from the spell of my promises. "I rather we stay in rubble than I lose my daughter. You say you offer me certainty, but I say I have certainty knowing I did not sacrifice Rose."

Damn his infantile mind! My fingers hungered for his neck. Confidence and trust be damned! The princess would just have to hate me.

Rose stepped between us. My anger cooled.

"This is insane!" she spat. "Do not torment him anymore. It's plain it is useless."

Her flame blazed brighter than his, and I found I desired it even more. She held a strong soul. A capable soul.

She turned and faced her father.

"I will not have you decide my fate. You've already done so once, and look what happened. My choice was taken from me, by you, and by those who terrorized and cursed me. I am taking my choice back. No one rules me but myself."

I chuckled inside. If only she knew the truth...

Rose faced me now.

"I will go with you, to protect and rebuild my kingdom. I won't have my family and friends, my people, harmed further because of me anymore. If my father isn't brave enough to take your deal, I will."

This was too much.

I handed her the parchment and quill. She opened it, her eyes scanning the scribbled and squished words.

"Sign at the bottom," I said, tapping beside the X.

"Don't do this!" her father shouted.

She didn't listen. Holding the quill tight between her thumb and forefinger, she scribbled her name, biting her lip as a line of crimson bled from the tip.

Euphoria. Rapture. Paradise.

All these flooded me as her blood sank into the contract, binding her to me. Letting me feast on her hopes and anguish, on her indescribable strength. I knew then why Fate wanted her. She was a woman to be reckoned with, and a soul that could hold the entire universe.

The king gripped her wrist and pulled it away, the quill falling to the floor, drops of her blood splattering on the stone.

"I won't allow this," he said, holding her.

I smiled.

"It's too late," I said, drunk on her. "The deal is made."

I held the contract out to him. He looked at his daughter, a mixture of sadness and anger fighting within him. I hoped what came next would help him understand.

I snapped my fingers.

A great wind blew in, swirling the dust into cyclones. Cobwebs peeled away, and split plaster smoothed and strengthened. Frescos and mosaics shone bright in reds, yellows, and greens.

The people kept their eyes shut as the wind swirled around them. The dirt lifted off their skin, and their hair returned to clean and tidy curls. Their togas covered them in color, and their jewels glinted once more.

The king himself didn't appear like the ghostly figure I had been conversing with. His complexion was healthy, and his crown shone bright. He smiled looking at his rings, and out over his court and home.

Repaired. Restored. Returned.

He was back home, and his eyes misted with joy.

"It's magnificent! Just as I remember," he said, his eyes bouncing from the walls to the ceiling. He embraced his daughter, and tears now fell down both their cheeks. "Though I can take no joy that this miracle came at your expense."

I was done with his emotional rubbish.

I turned away, making the contract disappear. Laila stood right before me, her arms crossed and face shallow. Sunken. Our eyes locked, and a sadness still hung within hers.

"She's so young," she whispered. "And she knows not what she does."

"No more than you did."

She nodded stiffly.

"We don't have a choice," I added.

"I know, it just brought me back to when I first saw you, that's all. When I... At least she is saving her family, instead of giving them away like I did."

I wanted to take her hand, but stopped when she looked behind me at someone. Tristan. He always had excellent timing.

"What did you make her sign?" he asked, his voice low.

I looked over my shoulder. Dammit. The members of the court stared, eyes wide and ears keen to listen to our little tete-a-tete no doubt. I put my hand on Tristan's shoulder, and brought him in closer to me.

"I did what I must to ensure she came with us, something you weren't able to accomplish," I breathed into his ear.

"Why didn't you tell her the truth at least before having her agree to such a bargain?" he asked. "She thinks she is going to defeat these sorceresses, when in fact that's who we want to find and release."

"I didn't tell her the truth for the same reason you obviously didn't," I replied, careful to keep my voice soft. I could almost feel the crowd's breath beating down on the back of my neck now.

His cheeks reddened as if shamed. He was still so innocent in the way the world worked. Naive to a fault.

I didn't like him feeling guilt for only doing what was best, even if morally gray.

"Tristan, listen to me. It's a kindness."

He raised an eyebrow.

"Really?" I could have done without the sarcasm in his tone.

"It's best to tell only what's necessary. Right now, before anything else, we need information from her. Think. What would make her more willing to share with us? Vengeance and a chance to be a hero, or knowing she is to release her tormentors from their prison? For Rose, it's easier to fight the threat you think, then what it really is."

"I don't like lying to her."

A woman broke from the crowd and took a step towards us, craning to hear any bit she could. Nosey shrew. I shot her a look of murder and malice. She stepped back with the others. Whispers now rose from them.

I hated these public spectacles.

"What would have have me tell her? That we are wanting to rescue those that cursed her to stop a mad god from enslaving all of humanity? Can you imagine her terror if she knew the truth?"

He crossed his arms as I pushed him aside. I went to Rose, extending my hand out to her.

The whispers from the court grew in strength and speed.

"It's time," I said.

She gave her father one last smile, then gave me her hand.

"Wait," he said. I groaned inside. "Have mercy. I beg you. I will not stand in your way any longer. I see now you bring greatness, and my daughter's bravery has helped me find my own."

"And? I haven't got all day."

"Can you allow me one night by my daughter's side? Now our home is repaired, our family and friends back together...it is unbearable to me to have her gone so soon. Can't we at least celebrate being reunited after a millennia of separation?"

"She will be back," I said, though I didn't really know that. "You can have all the parties you ever desired then."

He cleared his throat.

"If this curse has taught me anything, it is that nothing is certain. If you have any goodness in you, allow us this," he said. "Surely one night will not matter in your plans."

My palm burned, the scar feeling as if it was tearing into my bone. A night surely would matter.

I was about to tell him to go to hell, but Laila came to me, and pulled me to her. She leaned in to my ear, and I shivered as her hot breath curled across my cheek.

"Don't take her like this," she whispered.

"We don't have time to fritter away."

She bit her lip, casting her gaze to the girl, then back to me.

"We have time enough," she replied. "Let them have one night as a family. We wouldn't get more than two hours journey before nightfall anyway. It's excruciating being ripped away from everything you love."

I knew of what she spoke. I hated that memory. What I would give to forget the screams of the Furies that tore Laila from my grip. They were her punishment for breaking our deal, for simply wanting to choose her son.

I knew then I couldn't refuse her request. No matter how dangerous.

I released Rose.

"One night," I said.

Rose ran back to her father and embraced him, but Laila's smile is what melted my heart. It seemed she could always sway me in granting mercy.

I only wished I could shake the chill that I just agreed to a terrible mistake.

CHAPTER FOUR

I was shown to my apartments for the night, while Laila and Tristan were taken to their own private rooms.

Clay oil lamps flickered, covering pillows and rich carpets with a soft glow. Red silks and dark mahogany drowned me further in lush furnishings.

I closed and bolted the door, grateful for the solitude, any chance to be away from Laila.

I unrolled the lid to my flask and took a drink. If I couldn't harden my heart against her, whiskey could help make me numb. I hungered for numbness. Oblivion.

I threw my satchel on the bed and sat on the edge preparing to sink away. Lifting the bottle to my lips to drink again, I stopped.

My heart skipped a beat noticing a not wholly mediocre library of scrolls stacked on a far wall. At least I could spend the wasted time researching. Maybe some key information might be hidden within.

Putting the flask back away in my inner pocket I went up to the scrolls and rifled through them.

Mummies of the East. Interesting, but not useful. *Rivers and Oceans.* Pass.

Gods and Monsters. Not bad.

I slid the scroll out of its cubby hole and approached a heavy table by the window. Unrolling the parchment across the polished wood, I smiled at it being written in a language I knew. I hungered for any clue hidden within that might help us find Clotho and Lachesis.

Running my finger down the parchment I passed detailed etchings of werewolves, cyclopses, and women with snakes for hair, but I stopped at the word "vampire."

I chilled. Of all the creatures I ever encountered, the vampire was the most lethal. Not because of their strength, but because of their allure. Their prey confused fear with pleasure, forgetting reason entirely. Humans willingly fell into their deadly embrace, drawn to them as a fly to a sundew.

One particular vampire came to my mind, and fear rippled through my veins remembering him at all. We agreed to never cross paths again, and I hoped it would stay that way.

A knock at the door broke me from my thoughts. I sighed.

Opening the door a servant stood rubbing his thumbs against his fingers. He resembled a trembling puppy more than a middle-aged man. No doubt news of my leveling the king's guards reached his ears. I would be lying if I didn't say I was delighted in his fear of me.

"Sir, uh, great sorcerer, there is a feast being given and Prince Tristan explicitly asked for your attendance."

"Did he?" I asked, crossing my arms.

He quivered, then held out a wad of white material to me.

"What the devil is that for?"

"Festive dress. It's quite the celebration."

I laughed.

"I don't wear sheets, thanks."

He started to blubber, tripping over words that might convince me. I made to close the door in his face, but stopped.

A woman walked fast behind him. I couldn't help but let my gaze follow her float down the hall. Layers of crimson silk wrapped her slender form, half her chestnut hair piled in braids, the other half cascading past her shoulders. A silver headband of leaves crowned her head.

I pushed the servant out of the way, needing to see more of her. The woman turned. My breath stuck in my throat.

Laila.

Dressed in red, Laila was once more the regal woman who stood surrounded by mountains of straw waiting for me to destroy her.

I held out my arm to her like a common gentleman. I didn't realize what I did until it waited, hovering, for her to accept.

"Let me escort you," I said, pushing out the words despite my racing heart.

She looked as if considering my offer. Seconds passed, or minutes, I wasn't sure anymore as time ceased to exist.

She stepped back. I dropped my arm. Why had I been such a damn fool?

"I don't think it wise," she said.

"Why?"

Her gaze met mine and I found myself lost in her eyes.

"Please excuse me."

She turned away from me and continued down the hall at a fast pace, her gown of silk fanning out like flames behind her. They were nothing to the fire within my heart.

I returned to my rooms and closed my eyes in defeat as I shut the door.

Going back to the scroll I attempted to force my mind back on my task. But the harder I tried, the more my mind drifted away. After reading the same paragraph on minotaurs five times as I could not remember a word of it, I knew it was hopeless.

I unscrewed my flask again. A wave of sickness overtook me at the truth I tried to bury in drink. I was a broken man pining for the love of a broken woman.

Laila told me we could never be. Not because she didn't love me, but because her guilt was too great, and the pain from abandoning Tristan to me still fresh. Our love was not pure, but born of darkness.

There was truth in what she said, but why did it have to be this way? Couldn't two broken things help mend each other?

I believed myself drowning, gasping for air. I couldn't take it anymore.

I put the flask down on the table and stood, squaring my shoulders. I would not surrender. Not yet.

Opening the door, I swallowed down my fear and went after her.

TRISTAN

I read of feasts and celebrations, but no book ever prepared me for the rush of them. I wove between chatting men and women, careful not to step on their cascading togas or sandaled feet. A few others wore modern dress, no doubt curious neighbors. News spread fast.

Gold flashed as they raised their goblets to me, taking a drink in my honor and then bowing low in my wake. Their savior, the prince who rescued them from a vile curse.

I started to sweat, awkwardness churning in my gut. I only nodded in return, forcing an uneasy smile. Surely I deserved no such praise. I'd only kissed a princess.

Orange, sage, and cinnamon wafted through the air, followed by the mouthwatering scent of roasted boar. Turning to my right I passed a servant carrying a tray of parrot tongue pies, another held a large pitcher of wine.

He stopped before me and bowed, rising he mouthed something and held out a goblet to me. I couldn't hear a word over the horns and drums filling the space with music. I took the goblet, thinking he wanted me to admire it. He smiled, and poured wine into the cup, filling it to the brim. He retreated away, not hearing me as I called after him that I didn't want it.

I scanned the room, hoping for a place I could leave the goblet. My breath stuck in my throat. Rose stood dressed in a new gown of faint lavender, her eyes filled with life. She met my gaze and smiled, lifting her hand and waving to me. She then started to giggle. I realized why.

Wine rolled over the sides of my glass and dripped down my fingers. A pool of it lay at my feet.

I must have looked an idiot.

Cursing my stupidity I retreated back into the crowd. I didn't like her thinking me a dunce. Flinging the wine from my fingers onto the floor, I pushed my way through the crowd wanting to disappear.

More cheering and bowing heads met me as I pressed my way through.

"Hail Prince Tristan! Hail our savior!" they all chanted.

Awkwardness again rippled over me. Couldn't these people see I was an absolute fraud?

A bald man grabbed my hand, earnestness in his eyes.

"Thank you, prince. You've given me my life back."

I was about to tell him he was mistaken when a woman, hair a mess of curls, took my hand next.

"We would have all been lost without even knowing it, drowning in the darkness of sleep. But you've saved us from such a fate. From an eternity of nothingness. Your bravery is unmatched."

I supposed I had been brave...No. I shook the thought away. I wanted to believe them, but still I questioned if I had the right. I hadn't done much. Pater found the castle, Pater told me how to break the curse, all I did was happen to have the right blood.

A young child curtsied. Gold ringlets fell beside her rosy cheeks.

"Prince Tristan. You've made my mama and papa so happy. We would have been separated forever if not for you. You've saved my family."

Family.

That word melted my heart.

I looked around, this time with different eyes. All smiled, grateful- ness beaming from them.

I supposed I had helped them, reunited them and brought families torn apart back together. I knew the importance of family, especially after being reunited with my own mother. Family is all that truly mattered in life.

And because of family, my blood and my heritage, I alone could wake Rose from the curse. I laughed at myself for my earlier self doubts. Though I had no crown or kingdom, I was a prince, and I had helped others. That was enough.

With each step I grew bold. I felt warmth in my soul I never knew as they thanked me. I straightened my back and steadied my step. I lifted my goblet into the sky and cheers erupted. I smiled, then brought it to my lips and drank, celebrating what I was.

For the first time, I understood pride, and I found a desire to do more. I wanted to be a protector of the people. But what blazed within me more, was a need to safeguard my own people and lands.

It was my birthright, a life pursuing the welfare of others less fortunate. But Fate saw to it I never would have the legacy rightfully mine. Not to be revered, I didn't want that, but to help lead men. I could give them better lives, a feeling of safety within a kingdom of strength.

I curled my fingers into fists, resolute. Fate would pay for dethroning my father and casting me out. I would take back my crown. I would right the wrongs done to my people, and bring honor once more to the court. *My* court.

My thoughts were broken as a hush fell.

The king walked up to his throne and stood beside it, looking out. His toga of purple shone brilliantly against the glow of the torches and oil lamps.

"When the sorceresses came and foretold of Roses' fate, I didn't think we would ever celebrate in these halls again. Darkness and despair ruled us then, as we tried to find a way to escape the prophecy. We failed." He shook his head, as if traveling back to that time. "We owe all we are, and all we have, to Prince Tristan. May the gods ever bless him."

"May the gods ever bless him," everyone echoed.

He motioned for Rose to join him. Taking her hand, he patted it, his eyes filled with fatherly love.

For three seconds sorrow pitted in my gut that I would never know such a gaze from a father. I longed for such a connection. Though I had Pater, he wasn't my true father. That man was dead, and I hated Fate for taking him from me.

"Tristan, join me," the king said. He waved for me to come, the gold rings on his leathery fingers shining. My stomach tightened. What was he planning?

I stood beside him, close enough to Rose to catch her scent of jasmine and vanilla. My heart pounded for her.

"I wish you sit by my daughter and enjoy our thanks," he said. "Though you both must leave us tomorrow, I am grateful she will be in your care." His voice wavered, then he sucked in a breath. "But for tonight, let us not dwell on the past or the future, but live in the present."

Everyone clapped as he sat on his throne. I took the empty seat next to Rose, concentrating on the smallest radiation of heat from her arms and legs. She smiled, her lips soft and powdered pink. I wanted to kiss them again. I wanted to touch her satin skin.

I dug my nails into the chair instead, trying to restrain myself.

The king clapped, and recorders resumed lilting over the beating of drums. The exotic music pounded into my veins and down into my feet. Dancers leapt before us, lining up in two rows. Gold paint decorated their skin, and their hips swayed as they rang tiny cymbals on their fingertips.

My cheeks flushed as one dancer rolled her torso, her belly button peeking out of her skirts. Rose cleared her throat, and I realized my mouth was opened.

"Do people in this new age not enjoy such dancing?" she asked.

"They do, but usually they are more clothed, and dance with one another," I said. "It's less...provocative."

She furrowed her brow, as if confused.

"What do you mean 'together'?"

"Well, we dance with partners and mix and mingle. It is more intimate that way instead of watching others."

"Show me," she said.

My chest tightened, and I couldn't recall a single step Frau Latten had taught me. I wasn't going to let my fear stop me.

I took her hand, savoring her touch and led her to the floor. I placed her other on my shoulder, while I rested my own against her waist.

Her cheeks flushed.

"This is less provocative?" she asked, chuckling.

"Trust me," I said. "Move as I do and you will see."

I gave her a soft tug and off we went. Her pulse beat within my palm, and her breath heated my skin. A few clipped toes and apologies later, our legs fell in sync and we found our rhythm.

Her eyes brightened as we spun across the floor, but I loved her smile most of all.

"I feel like I'm floating," she said.

"Yes, it's much more pleasant dancing with a princess than with my old governess."

"You mean you've never danced with someone your own age before?"

Memories of dance lessons with Frau Latten washed over me. I shivered at the thought of holding her boney fingers.

"Pater, uh, Rumpelstiltskin, never allowed me to attend balls. I could only ever read about them in books, or learn the steps from my governess, who was about a hundred years old," I replied. "She smelled of shriveled plums, not at all like you. You smell amaz...sorry, I didn't mean to be imprudent."

Stop embarrassing yourself, Tristan!

She only giggled, and a wash of crimson covered her cheeks again.

"That sounds quite awful," she replied.

"Pater feared for my safety too much to let me out of his sight."

She nodded.

"I understand confinement due to a loved one's fears. Father never allowed me outside these castle walls. He meant only to protect me, but in the end, what good did it serve? It only kept me from experiencing the world I loved. He made me a prisoner."

I understood her completely. Pater did the same with me, and still I ended up with the threat of death in my future.

This made me hate involving her with Fate even more, especially when she just gained her freedom. No one deserved the cards dealt to her. Determination rushed through me that she would never know the fear of confinement again.

"I swear, you will never be a prisoner again after we defeat these sorceresses," I said, hating the half lie.

She squeezed my hand, and my blood heated. Something deep within me stirred and I dared to pull her closer.

Her eyelids fluttered and her lips reddened. Her breaths grew hotter and my heart thrashed in my ears. I leaned in, wanting to taste her again.

Applause erupted like thunder as the music ended, causing the spell enrapturing us to evaporate. She stepped back, and I sucked in a cooling breath.

Someone tapped my shoulder, and I wanted them to go away.

"I must compliment your dancing, your highness. You have your father's talent and light step."

Confusion swirled within me.

I turned and faced a man in his sixties. Gray hair waved around his sharp face. He wore fine clothes, though they were aged and outdated by twenty years.

"My father?"

"Of course, King Edward. How you've grown. You were only days old the last I saw you at your baptism."

I found myself speechless.

"Excuse me," Rose said. "My father is calling me, I'll return in a moment." She curtsied and left.

He bowed as she passed, then turned his gaze back to me. His lips spread into a smile, that while sincere somehow made me shiver.

"Allow me to introduce myself, my prince. I'm Lord Hochstein, Eighth Duke of Engleberg and once member of the court of your dear late father, the king. And, your godfather."

Godfather? My breath caught in my throat and excitement flooded me.

"I never knew I had a godfather. I actually, never knew who my real father was until recently."

"That's a true pity. He was a strong man," he replied. "We were close friends. Knew each other since we were lads. You are a spitting image of him, in fact."

I couldn't help but smile at this knowledge.

"It's hard to find anything about him. It seems all have forgotten my father," I said.

His face hardened.

"All except I, your grace. The rest are cowards. Gutless cowards. Your father ruled them well. Strategized to grow his kingdom for his people without a sword drawn. He was a great man, a great friend, and a better king. Until he came..."

His eyes fell on Pater as he sulked around the room. Pater's gaze was locked on mother. Lord Hochstein's lips tightened and he curled his fingers into fists.

A chill rolled down my spine.

"What does he have anything to do with my father?"

"Everything," he replied. "I saw that man once before. At the celebration of your birth. Your father loved you and spared no expense. You were wrapped in your mother's arms when he came and demanded she pay him what she owed. You."

Ridiculous as this sounded, I couldn't stop the hairs raising on the back of my neck.

"That's impossible. My mother and father were cursed by another. This man rescued her. He is no threat."

"Is that what they've told you? I suppose your mother wouldn't want you to know the truth." He chuckled. "This man, this *thing*, is the reason you don't have a crown on your head. He wanted it for himself, and your father's blood stains his hands. Don't let them fool you. "

My earlier chill dissipated, replaced by my blood boiling. I knew Pater was a man not to be crossed, but these accusations were insane. He sacrificed himself for our safety, and more importantly, I knew Mother would never protect a villain. She would never place me in harm.

"Sir, what you are insinuating is placing you on shaky ground. Let me remind you that most usurpers don't give up a kingdom once they've won it. This man has no crown. No title. Besides, my mother trusts him, and that is enough. I cannot fathom a woman protecting the man who murdered her own husband."

He shook his head.

"My prince, there is more to power than kingdoms," he said. "I only meant to warn you, and as your godfather, and subject, I am bound to protect you from the evil of others. You walk among wolves and I don't wish you to succumb to the same destiny as your father."

Though I hated his gall, I wanted to ask him more, about what destiny he spoke of, but Rose returned and grabbed my arm.

Lord Hochstein's expression immediately softened.

"My congratulations dear Princess." His words dripped with refinement. "Your story has long been told in these parts, and when I heard the news that the curse had been broken, I had to come and see for myself. I'm always glad to see monarchy reinstated and treated with the respect it deserves."

He cast me one final glance and left.

As I led Rose back to the dance floor, Pater leaned against a wall still staring at Mother. She glanced at him for a second or two, then returned back to her conversation with two other women.

Did their past twist together more than they let on?

Mother loved me. Pater sacrificed everything for both of us. They would never have used me as a bartering chip, or worse, killed my father. Any other notion was ridiculous.

Wasn't it?

RUMPELSTILTSKIN

I pressed my back against the wall and crossed my arms tight over my chest. No one approached me or tried to make inane conversation. In fact, they went out of their way to avoid me. I preferred it that way. I didn't like parties, especially after my last experience at one.

I hated the musicians plucking their lyres. I hated the roasted lion and pastries dripping with honey. I hated everything, except for Laila. She was the only reason I endured it at all.

Her eyes danced and sparked with a vibrancy I believed dead. Her lips pulled into a smile as she spoke to the woman beside her of horses and fine perfumes. The scent of citrus awakened in my memory as she pulled her fingers through her combed hair. Her laughter bubbled out and over the pulsing music.

My skin heated.

She lifted her gaze and our eyes met. My heart thrashed in my ears and I dared a step forward. She looked away, her attention back on the woman I now envied.

This was the seventh time she glanced at me, and hoped simmered in me that perhaps she was softening towards me.

Music throbbed in my veins and made me bold. I hungered to feel her against me once more, and what better way than with a dance? Surely she would accept my hand in light of the celebration.

I moved to touch her shoulder, but I let my hand fall back at my side. I didn't wish to touch her if she didn't desire it.

"Laila, I..."

She and the woman both looked at me, and my throat went dry. Words were my strength, my weapons, and now they all left me.

I became a mumbling idiot.

"If you aren't going to spit it out, then leave. You're interrupting a fascinating discussion of what hair trends are fashionable these days," the woman scolded me. I doubted Laila held her same fascination, as I had caught her yawning several times earlier.

"I didn't think you'd come," Laila said, her voice sounding disappointed.

Was my very presence so terrible to her?

"It's not every day one can experience an ancient feast," I pushed out. "But, that's not the reason I'm here. Laila, would..."

My throat tightened more, and I could only hear my own heart beat. What I wanted to ask suddenly seemed stupid.

I forced out my hand to her. Since words failed me, perhaps action could speak for me.

Her face relaxed and she gave a small smile. She reached out her hand. Relief washed over me that perhaps she would accept after all.

She retracted her hand, shaking her head.

"No."

"Why? Friends can dance, can't they?"

"But you know we are not friends."

"Then what are we?"

She bit her lip and twisted her gown in her fingers.

"Please, don't make this harder than it already is," she whispered.

"Fine, we don't have to dance. But can we at least speak?"

"I think you've spoken enough! Leave, you horrid man," the woman beside her snapped.

"Why don't you stuff your mouth with more marzipan, you old hag," I replied.

It took everything in me not to snap my fingers and seal her mouth shut.

Laila stood, glaring and pointing me to the door.

"It's ok, he is leaving," Laila told her.

I wasn't going to be bullied. I stepped closer to her, until her breath rolled hot across my cheeks.

"Laila, you keep shutting me out. I know we agreed, but. I...need you to know...Just, hear me out."

"Queen Laila, is this man bothering you?" a voice interrupted. A man's voice.

I turned, finding a man no more than thirty-five dressed in fine clothes from our own time. He seemed a typical rich man, charming and arrogant.

She forced a smile.

"He's only lamenting the lack of dance partners."

He chuckled.

"Yes, it seems not many know the Cinq Pas here. I don't suppose you'd do me the honor?"

He bowed to her, holding out his hand. I hated the relief that washed over her as she stood and took his arm, finally able to escape me.

"I'd be delighted," she said quickly.

He gave me a curt sneer as they passed me, moving towards the dance floor.

I bristled, but what else could I have expected? I cursed myself that I continued to be so ignorant. There would never be anything between us. She wanted our love dead and I had to kill the remaining embers still burning in the depths of my soul.

I slunk beside the wall, unable to turn my gaze from her with that man.

Her gown flowed around her feet as she danced. He placed his hand in hers and squeezed. Their heels pounded into the marble floor, their arms and fingers grazing each other with every step.

He was everything a young man ought to be. Vibrant. Young. Handsome.

For three seconds I wondered what it would be like to be him. I would hold Laila against my chest and our legs would intertwine with the dance. I would whisper in her ear and she would laugh. She would find me charming.

I laughed inwardly. Me. Charming. I only ever caused her pain.

We shared a dance once. I held her close, but only to intimidate her. I whispered in her ear, but only to threaten her. I made her cry, and she found me a monster.

I shook the memory away.

I couldn't survive like this. I was falling apart. I needed all my strength for what was to come, and now I was unraveling for a woman who didn't want my love.

I tore out of the room, leaving them all behind. I was tired. So tired.

My bondage to Fate deepened every day for her. She saw my goodness through the black. She let me taste salvation, to reach into the light, and now when I needed her most, she shut me out.

I entered my room and gripped the gnarled oak door and slammed it shut.

That was the problem. I felt too much now. It all ran through my veins and thrashed in my heart. Pain. Pleasure. Agony. Desire. All of it strengthened into a cacophony that threatened to sear my nerves and split me in two.

I needed the numbness to return. I needed to taste nothing. Hear nothing.

Feel nothing.

I shoved my hands into the maps and books on the table and pushed them all to the floor. Pots of ink spilled and splattered against the stone. Gripping the chair I hit it against the wall, the wood splintering easily.

Turning, I caught my reflection in a mirror of darkened silver. My chest rose and fell in great breaths, sweat glistening on my forehead. I hated what I saw. Weakness. Weakness because of love. Of being incapable of moving on. Of sentiment.

Gripping the oil lamp, I smashed it into the glass. Shards cut into my knuckles, but I didn't care. I thrived on their bite. Every sting removed me, gave me the pain I desperately needed.

I would reclaim what I was. Laila would disappear from my soul, and the monster would return. Cold hearted. Dead to the world.

I brought down my arm again, the mirror cracking and splitting. Glass exploded into clear pebbles at my feet.

I stopped and caught my breath. I uncurled my fingers from the lamp, allowing that too to break as it hit the floor. Drops of my own blood splattered the stone.

I ran my fingers through my hair, breathing in deeply and savoring the pain. Savoring the darkness. Savoring the oblivion. I had to in order to survive without her.

A clear *clink* of metal hitting stone rang out. It glinted in the torch light, and as I bent down to pick it up my heart stopped.

Laila's ring.

It had fallen out of my pocket. I trembled and my eyes burned, tears streaming down my cheeks. I leaned against the wall and slid down, burying my face in my hands.

I would never be free. I would never be the man I was. The moment I took that ring from Laila, the moment my heart first beat for her, there would never be enough pain in the world to erase her.

My palm split in agony. It tore into the flesh and bone. I screamed out, the sensations of being pulled and split intensifying.

"When will you ever learn sacrifice for love is overrated?"

I turned and my blood chilled.

Fate sat on the table, his legs dangling as if an amused child. Danger and beauty radiated from his hard features, and his white shirt fell half opened showing off his marble-like chest. But his wicked grin made me shiver.

"Beautiful room, isn't it?" he asked, sliding off the table. He picked up a vase with dancing figures, running his thumbs over the detail. "I remember when such furnishings were in fashion. They don't make cameo vases like this anymore."

"Why are you here?" I asked, my voice low.

He put the vase down on the table. I prayed he didn't see the books and scrolls laying open on the floor. I couldn't have him sniffing around and discovering our plan to cross him.

"I wanted to congratulate you on rescuing the princess, of course!" he said. "Pity the king isn't being accommodating. He always was an old goat."

"You wouldn't come all this way to simply congratulate me," I said.

He gave a small smile and looked down at the mess of scrolls. Sweat broke out across my brow. He bent down, and I prayed he didn't notice.

Laila's ring glinted between his fingers as he picked it up and held it out to me.

"You're right. I also wanted to check in. Make sure you are still honoring our agreement and not getting *distracted*," he said.

I took the ring from him, hating as our fingers grazed.

"I don't break deals."

He raised an eyebrow.

"Good. I really don't want to gut Tristan and risk staining my clothes." He stood right before me and leaned in. "And let us not forget I still have Laila's soul. My scissors haven't cut such a living thread in a millennia, and they hunger for her's."

He patted his pocket where he kept the thread he took out of Laila. One snip and she would be damned to nothing but a lost and tormented soul forever. I swallowed hard, and fear rippled down to my toes.

If he wanted to remind me of what we risked in disobeying him, he succeeded. Fully.

"If you're here to take Rose and I as your spinner and measurer, please just leave Laila and Tristan alone," I asked, almost begging.

Desire filled his face as he stroked my hair, as if imagining it all.

"As much as I might wish to take you now, I cannot whisk you both away." He let his hand fall to his side, and straightened his spine. "I have to rely on free will, on choice. Rose must come to me willingly. As must you. Otherwise that would be breaking the rules. And you know what happens when you break the rules."

Fate took out those scissors I hated and pulled them down my neck, letting the point press into my flesh. I shivered beneath the cold steel.

"But you can at least let Laila and Tristan go. They are of no more use to you now. You have what you want. You see I have done what you ask."

Fate cast another glance down at the scrolls on the floor, then back to me. He was clever, and he suspected.

"You have done nothing," he said. "Not until you are both truly mine will they be free. In the meantime, they are my insurance you will not do something stupid." He pressed against me, pushing me into the wall. He laid his hand over my heart, and my stomach twisted, hating the memory of the last time he touched me. "They are my insurance you will make the right choice and not cross me." He moved his hand lower, letting it slip in my trousers. "You remember how messy every-thing can get the moment choice is involved, don't you?"

I still hated myself for what I allowed to happen when I snuck into his kingdom in Dream. I allowed myself to fall into the warm embrace of a woman, only to be shown later it had been Fate tricking me all along. He wanted to show me how my free will, my choices, only made me a fool.

"Let go of me," I hissed.

"I grow impatient for you," he whispered. He stroked me, and I wanted to retch from the spark of pleasure he caused. "I look forward to when you are finally mine again. And if I catch a hint of you trying to thwart me, I will slice Tristan through and pull out his intestines and let them fall at your feet. I will squeeze his heart until it breaks. As for Laila, I hope you enjoy a woman's screams."

He evaporated before I could curse him, and I fell to the ground. Alone. Defeated.

I hurried to a side table and poured a goblet of wine. The goblet shook in my hands, and I drank heavily, the cedar and plum filling my mouth.

Fate's warning swirled in my mind.

I will slice Tristan through

Haze infected me as I drank deeply again. I fell into bed, desiring to sleep, but sleep wouldn't come. But I drifted, and in that drifting the malachite jar from Dream appeared again. And coming from it a sensation of needing. Wanting.

I hope you enjoy a woman's screams

I shivered. It's one thing to defy an enemy, it's another when you fully realize the consequences. For the first time, I truly feared. If we failed, torment awaited us all.

CHAPTER FIVE

Fell:

Verb: Stitch down (the edge of a seam) to lie flat

Verb: Knock down

TRISTAN

I tightened the harness of Rose's horse. Servants heaved bags filled with apples and dried meats over the saddles of the other three. Pater tucked away bottles of chianti and ale.

Mother spoke to Rose in serious whispers. Rose shook her head, and Mother's face turned grim. Pater approached them, and I strained my ears wanting to hear. Of course, I could easily guess of what they spoke.

The journey ahead of us would not be easy. The portal lay days away, and there would not be many villages we would pass through. Of course, this all relied on Rose's memories, of any information she could give us as to where we could find Fate's sisters. If she didn't remember...

A shadow fell over me. I turned, standing nearly eye to eye with Lord Hochstein. My insides bristled at his presence.

"Why are you here?" I asked.

He smiled, again true sincerity warming his features, though something behind it still made me uneasy.

"I wanted to wish you well on your journey," he said.

I resumed tightening the straps of the saddle. I didn't wish to hear anymore of what he had to say.

"I do not need your well wishes."

He touched my shoulder, and I couldn't stop from turning towards him again. His eyes bled with concern that gave me pause.

"You have your father's stubbornness," he said. "He would have been proud of you. You are discerning. That is a fine quality in a monarch."

I held my breath at the thought. To hear I had my father's pride was enough to swell my heart.

"Thank you," I replied, my throat dryer than I expected. "I wish I could have known him."

He nodded slowly, then reached out to stroke the horse's neck. He dove into his pocket and pulled out two cubes of sugar and fed it to the animal. Enso happily ate, seeming to delight in this man's generosity.

My shoulders relaxed.

"He was a good man. A proud man. He wanted only the best for you." He let his hand fall away back to his side. His features stiffened with emotion and earnestness. "I fear you and I got off on the wrong foot. I am not blessed with social graces. Age and bad times have gotten rid of what remained."

Guilt at my own suspicion overcame me. It was obvious this was a man who had endured a streak of bad luck.

"I don't enjoy the only father-figure I've ever known being dragged through the mud," I said, though this feeling surprised me. A month ago I wouldn't care if he called him a bastard, but time changed that.

"Of course," he replied. "But, don't disrespect your true father's memory by blinding yourself to the truth. If you will not take my word for it, perhaps you will take his."

He pressed a tattered book in my hands. Pages threatened to fall from the broken binding. Pieces of dried leather cracked and disintegrated.

Opening the cover, neat and tidy letters scrawled:

An Historical Account of the Rule of King Edward The Just, Written in His Own Words

Blood pounded in my ears. I rubbed my thumb over the fading ink of my father's own hand. I never thought I'd ever see something of his, and now I had his private thoughts and memories. What histories this treasure must contain!

I looked back up to thank Lord Hochstein, but instead Pater glared at me.

"What did that man want?" His voice was cold, frigid.

I snapped the book shut and buried it deep within my pockets.

"He was inquiring as to the breed of horse," I lied.

Pater's gaze narrowed.

"Don't speak to him again," he said. "We can't afford to have any nosey sorts interfering."

"I can decide to whom I speak, or don't speak," I spat.

He pressed his fingers against the bridge of his nose and shook his head.

"I don't want an argument. All I ask is for discretion until we get this all sorted out," he said. "That's it."

My father's journal pressed against my leg. Lord Hochstein's words ran through my mind. I wasn't sure if it was the rush of it all, or the irritation that Pater still treated me as a child, but I couldn't stop the shortness in my words. I couldn't stop the words at all, though I knew I should have.

"Unless this was all your plan from the beginning," I said. "Maybe you want the power being offered you. Maybe you want to spin the lives of others, you seem to enjoy controlling mine enough."

I regretted saying it immediately.

Pater's face sunk, and he remained silent. For the first time, he seemed truly hurt. A crow cawed in the distance, filling the space between us. I wanted to take back what I said, but I knew it impossible.

"I'm sorry," I whispered. "I..."

He waved, cutting me off.

"We have bigger problems than apologies," he said.

I raised my eyebrow.

"Such as?"

He sighed, and looked off into the distance. As if looking into a dark future.

"Rose doesn't know."

"What do you mean?"

"She has no memory of the sisters who cursed her. What they looked like, or what they said other than it was 'her destiny.' Your mother tried speaking to her, but...She can't help us, other than to continue the facade of taking her to Fate."

My guilt at what I said to him grew. Especially after a blow like this. We placed all our hope she would provide some clue, some precious information that might lead us to Fate's end.

"What do we do?" I asked.

"All we can do. Press on. I just don't like where we must go instead. I was hoping to avoid him, but we have no choice."

He grew paler than usual, as if marching towards his own execution.

"You are speaking in riddles," I said.

"Get Rose and let's get on with it," he growled. "There's no point discussing what's inevitable now."

I swallowed hard and went to retrieve her. I hated my thoughtlessness. Pater and I had our moments in the past, but he gave all for us. Determination renewed in me that we would vanquish this evil once and for all.

I pushed the poison of Lord Hochstein's words far away. I tried to ignore my father's diary pressing against my leg with every step.

Pater wasn't the evil one, it was Fate. It had always been Fate.

"It's time," I told Rose.

She embraced her father, and tears streamed down both their reddened cheeks. I hated the pain we put her in, the grief of leaving loved ones behind.

"I will fix this," she told the king, her voice cracking through her own tears. "The sorceresses will be defeated, and then we can finally live without fear."

I inwardly cursed myself that she still believed we were hunting the very women we wanted to save. I didn't like lying to her, but it was for the greater good. That made it ok, didn't it? I took solace in the fact the true evil would be brought to its knees.

She turned from her father, wiping her eyes. I took her arm and led her to her horse.

"I saddled her myself," I said.

She smiled, brushing her hand through its mane.

"I've missed riding. I love the wind skating across my skin and through my hair."

She placed her foot in the stirrup, but her joy melted away into horror. Her eyes froze on the metal jousting sticks decorating the saddle. They gleamed catching the sun, almost resembling needles.

"Do you not like jousting?"

"Jousting?"

"It's quite popular in our age. Two men race each other on horseback, armed with only shields and these long poles."

I tapped at the jousting sticks. She let out a breath, as if calming herself.

"You must forgive my nerves. I thought they were spindles."

Without thinking I touched her hand, and a spark of heat rippled through me. Our gaze held, and my heart hurt from the worry in her eyes.

"I will fetch you another saddle, if this one upsets you."

"No," she said. "If I am to succeed, I must conquer my demons."

She squeezed my hand. I could have died happy in that moment.

Her strength amazed me. After everything she'd been through, experienced, she still wanted to face her fears. I hoped for half her courage.

She sat on her horse and took the reins, giving a light kick with her heels into the animal's sides. I mounted my horse, as did Pater and Mother, and off we set after her at a steady pace.

Pater rode beside me, his steed of white a stark contrast to his black clothes and hair. Mother went on ahead next to Rose.

Remorse still festered in me from my angry words.

"About what I said earlier," I pressed out. "I didn't mean it."

He stiffened his lips, but nodded.

"I hope not. You and your mother are all I care about."

Were we always to be snipping and apologizing to the other?

"I know."

"That's all I want. For you to know."

He cleared his throat.

"She is a singular woman," he said, changing the subject.

I followed his eyes that now rested on Rose. My heart raced thinking of her.

"She is of a courageous spirit," I replied.

"Don't be a fool and take it for granted." His gaze flashed to Mother. "When you have love, you grasp it and hold onto it. You die for it."

The layers of this man were astounding. He could be cold and distant, then in a moment reveal a beating heart that seemed wounded and vulnerable.

He continued to stare at Mother, and something again scratched the back of my mind. Was there something deeper between them? Pater always spoke about the irritations of women, I couldn't ever see him settling down with one. Especially if that woman was my mother.

Unease twisted in me at the idea. Pater with my mother? Pah! I comforted myself that on the off chance he *did* have feelings for her, at least my mother didn't reciprocate.

I shook the mental images away, trying to save my stomach.

"Where are we going now that our plans have changed?" I asked.

His features turned grim. He paused before he answered.

"To find a being more dangerous than any we've yet faced."

❦

WE RODE FOR HALF A DAY, PASSING BY GENTLE ROLLING HILLS. THE movement of the horse worked my every muscle, and my back grew stiff.

If Rose suffered the same discomfort, I didn't know. Her face remained bright, and she looked with wonder at every tree or pond we rode beside.

"Where exactly are we headed?" she asked.

My heart raced at her voice, grateful for conversation. Anything to take my mind off the cramps in my legs.

"To find someone who might know where the sorceresses are hiding."

At least it was the truth this time.

Silence again. I tapped my fingers against my reins, wanting to say something more, but without a thought of what that could possibly be.

I opened my mouth planning to ask her about the rare maps that might be in her library, when she cleared her throat. I shut my lips. It was probably for the best.

"I've discovered that what they did to me has become a sort of legend, but what of you?" she asked. "You mentioned these vile creatures destroyed your family. That they killed your father? I can't even imagine the loss you suffer."

My father's journal still pressed against my leg, a comforting reminder that he was with me on this mission, in a way.

"I was only a baby when it happened. It's hard to grieve for a man I never knew, but I do grieve for the moments I was never allowed to have. Watching you and your father reminded me of what they robbed from me."

"I've also lost a parent. The pain never truly goes away. You are lucky to still have your mother. I miss my own every day."

"I hadn't a mother until recently. Having her back in my life is a blessing, like finding a missing part of myself. I know who I am, and where I come from."

She smiled, then bit her lip, as if thinking of something more to ask me.

"If you can excuse my impertinence, she looks very young to be your mother. You are almost the same age."

I hoped she didn't notice the sweat breaking out on my temples.

"The sorceresses imprisoned her for nineteen years in a realm without time." At least it was still a half truth. "That's why she hasn't aged. They took her from me when I was days old. They murdered my father. I hate them."

Pain bit the back of my throat. The emotion of it all seemed to cascade over me. Rose frowned and shook her head.

"They are monsters. Truly monsters."

"This is what presses me to end their terror. They took from you, and they took from me, from my mother. But I will not let them take from another."

Fire burned in me for Fate's neck. He had made me an orphan, and laughed at us pawns as he played his twisted game.

"Are you afraid?" she asked.

I let several seconds slip by before I answered. "I'm terrified."

If only she knew the whole truth of the question she asked. I wanted to tell her, to beg her to run and hide, but it would only make it worse for us all.

The thought of our failure sent a sickening chill down my spine.

I could feel Fate's blade ripping into my gut. I could feel the twisting agony as he tore out my intestines. I could feel him cracking into my chest, gripping my heart and squeezing.

I shivered at the thought of the pain, of the gnawing, raw agony as he split and broke my body.

But there was no going back now. There was only forward.

"What of your story?" I asked, wanting to change the subject. Anything to get my mind off of the knot in my stomach. "I mean, I know your story, but legend and truth are often quite different."

She pressed her lips together. Her cheeks flushed, but she rolled back her shoulders, as if willing a great strength to fill her.

"The truth is, I was a fool. A selfish fool."

"That can't be true."

"It is," she replied. "I placed my own desires above everyone else. All I had to do was not touch the spindle, but I couldn't even do that. It called to me, and how pretty its words. The sensation, the spinning wheel, became more important than my father. Than my entire kingdom. I touched it. I willingly damned everyone and let it prick my skin."

I swallowed hard.

"The spindle was enchanted. There was little you could do."

She shook her head.

"No, I had a choice and I was weak. I didn't want to refuse," she said. "That is why I must fight now. I must right my wrongs and take back what I stupidly gave away."

I sensed her anger at herself. I didn't like the guilt she openly carried on her shoulders.

"We will conquer," I said, not knowing what else I could say.

"I failed once before, what's to say I won't again?"

Though her fortitude was strong, below existed a wasteland of shame and uncertainty. I couldn't let her be eaten by self doubt.

"You said it's a choice. You are making the choice now to fight, to continue on. Our resolve is all we have and if we persist, if we keep the course, we do not fail. You will not fail."

She smiled, and the storms behind her eyes cleared.

"I hope you're right."

I wanted to reach out and stroke her cheek, to let her know it would be ok, even though I wasn't sure myself.

"The horses need water and rest," Pater's voice cut through.

I cursed Pater internally. He always knew how to break a moment.

We dismounted, and directed our horses towards a nearby stream. They drank happily as I stretched my legs. Rose came next to me, and I couldn't help but close my eyes as I caught the scent of vanilla rising from her skin.

"You've told me of you and your mother, but what of him?" She motioned towards Pater.

He sat on a stone, drinking from a silver flask. His eyes kept darting to Mother who had her face buried between the pages of a book. She always seemed to keep herself distracted around him.

"He's the man who raised me," I said. "I owe him a great deal. He took me in, gave me an education, and kept my stomach full. We don't agree on much, but he is protective of those he loves. I respect that about him."

"He looks lost," she said.

He stood and fed his horse an apple. Mother glanced at him, but when he turned around she quickly returned to her book. He took another drink from his flask as he passed by her.

I suppose he did look more miserable, but then he always looked miserable.

"Don't worry about him," I said. "He is too complicated to figure out."

She chuckled.

"How is he and your mother connected?"

"They...well...she and he...no..." I had no clue. "He saved her from her imprisonment and reunited us. I'm afraid I know nothing of their history. He would never speak but a few vague sentences about my mother when I grew up. I assume they are no more than acquaintances, and barely even that based on how they behave around one another."

She looked at them again, a touch of pity seeming to define the soft lines of her face.

"Acquaintances don't usually risk life and limb for the other. There's always a story, and theirs looks particularly deep."

You were wrapped in your mother's arms when he came and demanded she pay him what she owed. You.

The hairs rose on my neck again as Lord Hochstein's voice echoed in my mind.

Pater handed Mother a wineskin filled with chianti. Her cheeks flushed as she took it from him, refraining from any eye contact. He remained, as if wanting to say something to her. She turned the pages of her book with greater force. His shoulders sunk and his features hallowed. For a second he looked like a broken puppy, but he hid it quickly behind a mask of indifference. Lengthening his spine, he returned to his rock.

Was I so blind to the truth? Or, was it just unfounded conjecture?

My father's diary pressed harder against my leg. It pulsed, as if telling me that inside its pages rested the truth. I pulled it out and stared at the cover.

"Tristan," Mother called. "I have some cakes for you and Rose that aren't completely crumbled."

She smiled, her eyes shining with love. My heart grew, and I didn't know if I wanted the truth. I didn't want to give into suspicion. I didn't want to distrust the mother I waited so long to have.

I slipped the diary back in my pocket, but the questions swirling in my mind remained.

I knew I couldn't ignore them much longer.

CHAPTER SIX

RUMPELSTILTSKIN

A **gaggle of** geese squawked as we rode into a village of tight streets and alleys. I sensed his presence among the leaning plaster houses and coarse men. He was always desperate for his master, and this desperation was the weakness I needed to find him.

I pulled on the reins, directing my horse to the left following the trail.

The stench of need grew stronger. Stifling.

A flash of yellow silk. A glint of a silver tipped cane. An explosion of a yearning flame. His flame, his soul.

I smiled as he entered a bank and soon emerged pocketing his embroidered purse. Fine thing. A gift, no doubt, for services rendered.

He bowed low as two ladies walked by, lifting his gaze once they passed to admire their backsides. His lips curled into an oily grin that sickened me.

He brushed dust off his canary doublet, and straightened his gold buttons.

"I don't like this," Laila whispered to me.

"We have no other option," I replied.

Disgust twisted her features watching him twirl his mustache into fine points. God, I loved this woman.

"Can we trust him?"

"Only if we persuade him."

She grimaced, and shot me a warning look.

"That's what worries me. I know how you persuade," she said.

"At least I get results."

She didn't seem impressed with my answer.

He slipped inside a tavern, and I knew it was time. As did Laila. She rubbed her neck, as if nervous.

"Won't your *persuasion* techniques add tension between us all? Make him ask questions? Questions we don't want him asking?"

My stomach pitted at the thought.

If Tristan ever discovered our past, what truly happened, I doubted he would remain by our sides. Dread filled me at the prospect of losing him. But while the fear of Tristan hating me again sickened me to my core, the fear of him hating his own mother was unacceptable to me.

"Don't worry. I intend to go alone. He won't see the monster I am. I can't have him see."

Emotion overtook her face, but what emotion I wasn't sure. Confusion, perhaps? I knew it wasn't pity.

Was it?

"You aren't a monster," she said. "Not any more."

My pulse quickened.

"Yet you still look away every time I enter a room."

"What other choice do I have? You don't know the torment I suffer when I'm near you."

"I know it all too well. It's the same I suffer when I'm not near you."

Her gaze searched me, deepening into my own. Irritation faded into need. Want. She wet her lips, and an overwhelming desire to kiss them blazed in me. We hadn't looked at each other with such intensity since the night we shared.

That night. It still sent shivers through my blood.

Tristan's horse clopped beside us shattering the spell. I cleared my throat and Laila shifted in her saddle.

"What are you two whispering about?" he prodded.

"Nothing," Laila replied, a bit too quickly.

He raised an eyebrow.

"We are discussing the old acquaintance I am to call on," I replied.

"An acquaintance like you and Mother are?" he asked, almost snidely.

I would never figure out what made that boy tick.

"No, more like a sick bastard I always hoped would choke on his sugared plums. But, he is the only link to finding the being we need, who is far worse. Darius."

He seemed to relax slightly at my sharing this information.

"Darius? You mean the one you spoke to me of?"

I nodded.

"We made a vow to stay out of each other's way, and I am about to break that vow. I don't expect a warm reunion."

We dismounted our horses and tied their reins to a post.

"Wait here. This shouldn't take long," I said to the group.

"No." Tristan gripped my wrist, but immediately let me go as if realizing his mistake. I was used to him arguing with me, but he'd never been so aggressive.

"I don't require an escort," I snapped.

"I will go with you. I insist," he pressed.

"I will go, too," Rose announced, stepping towards us. "If this will help save my kingdom, then I demand a part in it."

I pulled my hand down my face. Great. Just what I needed. Two obnoxious youths badgering me.

"That is unwise, princess," I growled.

"Is there a reason you want to go alone?" Tristan cut in. "Is there something you don't want discovered?"

For a flash he looked at me as if a traitor, but it disappeared before I blinked. What had gotten into him? His behavior unnerved me. Hurt me, which upset me most of all.

"You still don't trust me?" I asked.

He paused. I didn't like pauses. They always said everything

"It's not that," he said. "It's because we agreed to do this together. Not alone."

He stared at me and I tried to search for the lie I knew resided beneath.

"I'm only protecting you. That thing is a creature that serves a monster hell doesn't even want," I said.

"I don't need protecting anymore," he replied.

"Nor do I," Rose followed.

"If we trust each other, as we claim, then we must do this as a team," he said. "It's not right you always put the burden on yourself."

I sensed the eyes of others on us now. I couldn't risk that silk clad fool running out the back from hearing our raising voices. I was running out of options, and gagging Tristan was sadly not among them.

"Together, then," Laila cut in. "We will all go together."

"But..."

"This is how it must be," she interrupted. "No more arguing, or else we fail before even getting through the door."

Anxiety etched her face.

It reflected my own.

❦

FLOORBOARDS GROANED BENEATH OUR FEET, AND MY SOLES STUCK TO the splatters of ale and whiskey.

His oily presence radiated from the back room. Grabbing a brass handle I opened the door to a private room, ducking beneath the low frame.

Dark timber and smoke pressed in on us. Tall windows accentuated his short stature as he looked out over the bustling townspeople below.

"Mishkin," I said.

He turned, the shadows continuing to shade him. Only the elegant lines of his slender shoulders and legs were visible. His master kept him looking like a pristine doll.

"Still sneaking about I see," he said, his voice smooth and patronizing. "But we have friends, now! I must say, I'm surprised at you, Rumple. I never pegged you as the social type."

He reminded me how much I hated him.

"I've not come to chat."

He sneered.

"Master will not be pleased you've come at all," he replied. "He won't appreciate you mixing him up in your spot of trouble. Don't look so shocked, it's beneath you. You know news travels fast in our circles."

He walked into the light and poured himself a brandy. My breath caught in my throat. Lace barely hid the scabs and bite marks covering his hands and wrists. His thick cravat obscured most of the wounds around his neck, but not all.

Rose gasped, and his gaze found her behind me. His mouth twisted into a nasty smirk.

"And you must be the princess wanting to rectify what you allowed torn asunder."

She stepped forward, though she quivered.

"I will fix what I let be destroyed. Mark me."

Her strength impressed me, but I didn't like the laughing glint that woke within his eyes.

"My master remembers your father's idiotic plan to destroy all those spinning wheels. Didn't do much good. You couldn't keep your fingers off those shiny baubles, could you?"

He sipped his brandy.

"How dare you!" Tristan yelled, lunging at him.

I put out my arm, holding him back.

Mishkin only laughed.

"I am disappointed in you, Rumple. A man of your talents shouldn't keep such dismal company. A fallen queen, a lost prince, a princess who couldn't listen. You are the most peculiar band of misfits I've ever seen."

I burst towards him, gripping his neck and crushing him against the molding plaster. His brandy glass fell and splintered at our feet.

"I disappoint you, do I? Do not forget with whom you deal," I hissed.

"And don't you forget with whom *you* deal," he croaked.

I tightened my grip. I would not be shaken by his warning, though I knew I should.

"Where is your master hiding these days?" I asked.

"Not telling."

The little shit.

I pressed harder into his neck, my fingers squeezing into his muscle. His tongue lolled out of his mouth and I couldn't help but smile as his skin took on a lovely shade of blue.

"I'm not a patient man. If you don't give me what I want, I will make you plead for death."

He gave a raspy chuckle, as if unfazed. Magic guarded him from me, but his master's protections weren't strong enough if I kept squeezing.

I pressed my nails harder into his throat.

"Stop! You're hurting him," Rose said.

"That's the point," I growled. He gasped for air now, and his eyes bulged.

"This is madness! Surely there's another way?" Tristan said. "Something more civilized?"

"And what do you suggest? Sing him lullabies? Give him sweets and hope he'll be nice?"

"I have no problem with force, but this is torment," he said.

Revulsion filled Tristan's eyes. My enjoyment in Mishkin's pain evaporated. I hated the horror I inspired in him. I took care he never knew the truth of my dark dealings. Now he saw it all in its raw terror.

What I feared turned truth. He realized I was a monster.

I let Mishkin go and he collapsed to the floor, choking and coughing.

I sucked in a breath to help dampen my rage. Tristan nodded in thanks. That boy would be my undoing.

I knelt down and sat Mishkin against the wall.

"Perhaps I've not tried the right way with you. I can offer you anything you want. Surely there must be a life you would prefer to live?"

"Go to hell," he rasped.

I chuckled. They always fought me.

"I am your savior. I can grant you peace. Let you rule your own life, instead of running errands for a demon."

I hoped I could get through and tempt him. Not for his sake, but for my own. For Tristan.

He remained silent. My right eye twitched.

I grasped his chest, searching for the despair within him I sought. I wanted it. Needed it. His flame burned, but not for me. Only for him. His master, Darius.

A vampire.

Vile creatures. They infected their slaves, creating a drone whose heart beat only for their needs. But Mishkin was a man, and all men were weak. There had to be something in him I could use. Anything to seduce him to reveal his master's location.

Searching deeper I raced through hunger and thirst, past desire and recognition, to the pulsing beat at Mishkin's core. Every soul contained a seed of selfishness, something that I could use to turn even the most humble into greedy animals.

Still, nothing.

I pressed my eyes harder shut, trying to concentrate on excavating his depths. His cravings.

Darius was his craving. His only craving.

My hatred of vampires grew. How could they erase a man so completely?

"Have an original wish, Mishkin!" I yelled. "I offer you the world, and you only want to remain a slave."

He spit in my face. I ground my teeth and let him go, wiping it away.

"Fuck you," he croaked. "You deserve the misery waiting to embrace you forever. My master and I will laugh as your carcasses rot at destiny's door."

I glared at him. Everything in me chanted to kill him, to squash him like the disgusting insect he was, but Tristan's disapproving face kept me frozen. For the first time I was incapable, unable to do what I must.

I couldn't risk losing Tristan, but I also couldn't risk damning us all if I failed to find Darius. Since Rose could remember nothing of value, he was our only hope to end Fate.

A hand touched my shoulder. I turned, Laila standing by my side. Her eyes bled with resolve, and with fear. I understood.

"There is no other way," she whispered. She squeezed my shoulder, before letting her hand slip back to her side. "We can't go back now."

She turned to Tristan. Rose's skin grew pale.

"Sometimes we must do what we hate for the greater good," she told him. "If this creature is what stands between your life or death, then it must be done. I'm protecting you as I always should have."

He cocked his head in confusion.

"Always should have?" he asked.

"Forgive us," she replied.

Laila's gaze met mine again. A fire blazed in her eyes I hadn't seen since she first decided to grasp the crown for herself. It enthralled me and heat washed down my legs.

"Do what you must. Destroy him," she ground out. "You've tried to reason, now is the time for blood."

I prayed Tristan would understand. A parent must keep their children safe, no matter the cost. I, *we*, couldn't let Fate win, not when we already came so far.

I turned to Mishkin. A shiver rolled down him, but it was nothing to the chill in my own veins knowing what I must do.

"I was a fool to offer you your heart's desire when I see you already have it. So I am going to take instead. I am going to take what you want most. I am going to steal what you want most to give, then perhaps you will accommodate."

His face twisted with confusion. Then, agony.

"STOP IT!" Tristan screamed, but I forced his protestations away. There was only I and Mishkin in the room.

His rounded cheeks sunk, and his plump fingers curled. The pink hue of his skin turned gray ash. He cried out, but even his voice withered into hacking coughs.

He trembled violently.

"Wha...what have you done?" he wheezed.

"Save your voice, Mishkin. Otherwise you won't have much strength left. In fact, you haven't much *life* left."

He clawed at his chest, his fingers brittle and boney. I despised myself for how much I loved watching the realization filling him with horror.

"Where is it?" he asked.

"Your heart?" I chuckled. "I took it. I took everything, every last drop of blood you wish for your master. He savors you slowly, like a fine port. Only a taste here, a suckle there. Never enough to truly drain you, of course. Not yet, not until your usefulness wanes and he craves the true prize. Your heart. That final, precious beat."

"Let me...have...it back! I promised...him!"

"It's the greatest gift a servant can offer a master. Only then will he reward you to be like him. Timeless. Immortal."

His eyes flared with hatred. He grunted as if trying to curse me, but his tongue wilted rendering him incapable.

"This should be quite simple, Mishkin. You either tell me where Darius is, or I will leave you here to shrivel into a mummified corpse."

His white skin cracked like taught leather as he trembled. He opened his mouth, the corners of his lips splitting as he gasped for air. His lungs were no doubt parched bags. No relief would come to him until I allowed it.

I bent down closer.

"Shhh...don't try too hard. You have mere minutes if you are lucky until your repulsive life ceases."

I pressed against his ribs again, his skin rough and dry, deprived of life. I hunted for the answer I wanted.

Desperation. Fear. Hope.

Surrender.

Everything I wanted burned in him now.

"Do we have a deal? Your master's whereabouts for your precious heart and blood?"

He closed his eyes, his one lid snapping off. A strong "yes" flamed in his soul.

I smiled.

"I knew Darius wouldn't choose a complete idiot," I said.

I waved my hands and his skin turned pink and the cracks on his lips healed. His cheeks plumped and he coughed in deep breaths.

"You fucking bastard!" he hissed.

I rolled my eyes.

"Your anger is of no interest to me. We made a deal, now tell me where Darius is, unless you want me to return you to your previous state."

He ground his teeth, his eyes never leaving mine. His hatred burned fierce. I was impressed by its intensity.

"He's in Regensburg. He lives beneath the church, among the dead things."

Of course he would.

"Thank you. It's always entertaining when our paths cross," I quipped.

Satisfied with myself, I turned back to the others.

Laila's features darkened, and her chest rose and fell in deep breaths. She stood taller, and strength radiated from her. I fell into the past, when we both stood alone in Edward's dungeon. When she vowed to break him, to take back her power through her pain.

I wanted to kiss her back then, I had kissed her, and I wanted to kiss her now.

But my smile fell to a solemn grimace. Tristan held Rose who whimpered in his arms. Disappointment, no, disgust, filled his face.

My heart sunk.

"What are you?" he asked.

"Someone who does what's necessary to keep those he loves safe," I replied.

He shook his head.

"No, such force is never necessary."

"Tristan, please understand," Laila said. She reached out to him, but he pulled away.

"I'm taking Rose out," he said, walking her to the door. "I need a minute alone. From both of you."

They left.

"Have we lost him?" I whispered to her.

"Tristan is intelligent. Give him time, and he will come around. He's so young, and has experienced so little of the world. How the world really works."

"Do you believe that?"

"He's safe, and that's what matters," she said, not answering. "I don't want him to hate me, to find out...but I had to put him above my own needs for once. If he hates me, then at least it was in the effort of saving him."

I tried to take her hand, but she pulled away. What else did I expect?

"We need to go," I said.

Opening the door Mishkin's voice croaked behind us.

"Fools," he rasped. "You still think you can escape Fate? I saw the scar on your hand, Rumpelstiltskin. It's deeper now. What you did cannot be undone. The choices we make in the dark can never be escaped."

He laughed and my palm burned, pain searing into my bones and sinew. I closed my fist tight, swallowing down the agony.

"We shall see," I said.

CHAPTER SEVEN

Tow:

Noun: Short or broken fiber (as of flax, hemp, or synthetic material) that is used especially for yarn, twine, or stuffing

Noun: Accompanying or following usually as an attending or dependent party

LAILA

At nightfall we reached the small town of Bregins and secured rooms. Gratefulness filled me to finally be able to distance myself from the others. Well, from one in particular.

I stared into the fire, trying to dissolve the sensations Rumpelstiltskin awoke in my blood. Seeing his power and danger again made me quiver. I hated how that danger enthralled me. Captivated me.

Thrilled me.

Mortification pitted my stomach at my weakness. I didn't want him. I shouldn't want him.

Especially as I held my son's anger. When Tristan looked at me now, disillusion hardened his expression. Him knowing what I was capable of humiliated me.

How much worse would it be if he knew I still hungered for the man I willingly sold him to?

I couldn't bear the thought.

Tristan finally spoke a few tense words to me, of forgiveness and moving on. But a wall remained, and I hoped in time he would remove the bricks.

I knew if I wanted my son, I couldn't risk any further disquiet. That meant banishing my desire for Rumpelstiltskin.

I did want him.

I shoved my face in my hands, demanding all thoughts of him clear. The fire popped and split, as if cackling at me. My mind centered stronger on him.

He stood over Mishkin, his eyes lit with malice and power. Again he was the man I first met nineteen years ago that captured my imagination and my heart. The stranger that broke into my world and shattered it at my request.

I knew he wasn't the same man as back then. Nor was I the same woman. But that didn't change the choices we made. Every lie and every twist in our souls would be ours forever. We were monsters among pretty things.

Mishkin was right. We could never escape our choices made in the dark.

"Laila."

My heart raced hearing Rumpelstiltskin's voice. Why did he have to come now?

I pulled my hands down my face and focused on his. His cheeks angled into a pointed chin, and his gray eyes still stormed as always. Wicked grace and angelic beauty were at one in this man. I begged my heart to slow, but it refused.

He pressed his thumbs into his palms.

"I know you rather I not disturb you," he whispered. "But I felt compelled to thank you for...back there."

"What do you mean?" I kept my voice low. I didn't want Tristan overhearing as he sulked in a back corner with his maps.

"For sharing in Tristan's disappointment. I am used to being the one entirely to blame." He paused, as if bewildered. "It's nice to not be alone, for once. You gave me the strength I needed to do what we must."

"We've been through too much together. I won't let you falter," I replied.

"Nor I you," he said.

His gaze fell to my shoulder and he reached out to me. His fingers brushed my skin and I hoped he didn't notice I closed my eyes. He retracted his hand, holding a thread. The fire glowed off the white fibers shading it in gold.

Golden thread. I loved watching how it had spun through his fingers that first night he came to me...

Damn my heart!

I looked away, not allowing myself to fall into him again.

My gaze found Tristan's. My throat went dry as his brow furrowed, but he snapped his attention back to his maps.

Guilt inflamed my cheeks.

"I think it best you go, now," I whispered, so low I didn't even know if he could hear me. "I don't want a repeat of earlier." That wasn't the only reason I wanted him gone. I couldn't contain myself much longer around him.

Rumpelstiltskin cleared his throat. He straightened his doublet and combed his fingers through his black hair.

He dropped the thread, letting it float down to our feet.

"I'll slip away before he has time to notice."

"Be safe," I said, surprised by my worry.

His lips pulled into a sad smile, and fear bled through his eyes. I'd never seen him fear so greatly before.

"I wish I could promise you."

※

HOURS PASSED.

I pulled my finger down the page of my book *Ancient Mysteries*. An answer or hint must be in one of the sentences hidden among the other thousand.

I knew Rumpelstiltskin favored action, but I favored not putting all our faith in one being. Darius might hold more knowledge than any other, but we thought the same of Rose. We couldn't risk more failures.

Time was running out. The blood moon was tomorrow, and still we were no closer to gaining our freedom.

I rubbed my chest over the place where Fate had pulled out my life's thread. My soul. The hairs on my arms and neck raised at the thought of him still possessing it. Knowing that at any moment he could cut it with his scissors.

Then, there wouldn't be darkness, there would only be torment.

Determination swelled in me stronger than ever. We would find Clotho and Lachesis. Fate would be finished.

I flipped past passages of hexes and diagrams of constellations. Flipped past incantations, rivers of fire, an illustration of a malachite urn.

My eyes burned from reading. I lifted my gaze and blinked away the dryness.

Warmth filled me as Tristan and Rose spoke by the fire. He reached out to her, moving a lock of her hair behind her ear. She smiled for a second or two, until her expression fell somber, as if something worried her. I could easily guess what.

She had not fared well after the events with Mishkin. She refused to eat, and preferred staring out the window. Though great bravery filled her heart, it was crippled by self doubt.

I knew the sentiment, having faced it myself when I was trapped in Edward's dungeon.

He took her hand, holding it securely. He spoke more earnestly, but about what I couldn't hear. I appreciated his concern and tending of her.

Pride filled me at the man my son became. Though he resembled his father, he didn't have his cruelty. Tristan was gentle and kind, everything Edward wasn't.

This relieved me greatly.

He got up and laid a blanket across Rose's shoulders. His fingers grazed her cheek. She looked at him deeply. I knew that look.

She was falling in love with him, and he with her.

I couldn't help a flush of envy.

I glanced at my feet. The thread Rumpelstiltskin had dropped earlier still glowed in the firelight. I bent forward and picked it up. The fibers curled together, the ends frayed and mangled.

A love like Tristan and Rose's would never be ours. Our love was twisted, just as the thread Rumpelstiltskin spun, just as the thread I now held.

I neared the fire and let it dangle over the flames. What I wanted I could not have. It only caused grief. It was wrong.

I dropped the thread into the flames, the fire consuming what ought never to have existed.

Sobs broke over the spit and pop of the fire. At first I thought they were my own, but I turned to Tristan holding Rose. Redness flushed her cheeks, and tears trickled down them.

I held back my own tears that threatened to fall for the man I should never have wanted.

TRISTAN

"I'm going to fail," Rose said. "Mishkin is right. I can't listen. I will sabotage you, just as I did my family. I'm incapable of anything else."

"Don't let that mad man's words infect you," I said. "I've never met a more capable woman."

She chuckled through her tears.

"A capable woman wouldn't fall apart from a few mean words." She took in a breath, trying to calm herself. "I shouldn't be so upset, but he awoke fears within me. Thoughts keep swirling in my mind, telling me I will fail. That I can't do it. I know they are wrong, but they keep speaking to me. And I can't stop listening."

I lifted her hand to my lips and kissed it, wanting to reassure her.

"You are not alone this time," I said. "You have us. You have me."

She rubbed her thumb over my knuckles, and squeezed my palm.

"When we first started out, I believed in myself. I knew I would right my mistakes. But now?" She released my hands, as if I shouldn't be touched. "Today showed me I only lied to myself about my strength. I lied to you. Your mother is the capable one, not me."

My mother's face flashed in my memory. Danger gleamed in her eyes that chilled me to my core. Her lips had spread into a smile, a satisfied thrill overtaking her. I'd never seen that woman before. I didn't want to see her again.

"That's not true." Rose didn't find pleasure in the torment of others as my mother apparently did.

The odd business between Mother and Pater kept spiraling. Mother constantly whispered in Pater's ear. Hunger grew in their gazes for the other. I could no longer deny they shared some connection that went deeper than everything.

Do you even know who this man, this thing, *really is? He is the reason you don't have a crown on your head. He wanted it for himself, and your father's blood stains his hands*, Lord Hochstein's voice echoed.

The whole thing started to make me ill the more I thought about it. I wanted to push it away. To ignore it as drivel...but it kept coming back, each time growing louder than the last.

Then, with Mishkin...

Rose shook her head.

"She was able to do what was necessary to protect you. To protect us. She didn't whimper. She didn't cower like me. I don't know if I can show that power when we face the sorceresses."

You walk among wolves.

"What's wrong?" Mother asked, her voice cutting through my thoughts. I couldn't help but tense.

"Rose is having doubts," I replied.

"About what?"

"Herself."

Mother looked at Rose and a pitying smile pulled on her lips.

"Tristan, why don't you give me some time alone with her? We need to speak woman to woman."

Words stuck in my throat as my mind raced. Was I really afraid of leaving Rose alone with my own Mother? The woman who until today I trusted above all others?

This was insane.

My father's journal pressed against my leg, and I heard it call to me again. That it could put all these demons to rest.

That it could tell me what I always should have known.

The truth.

"Of course," I pushed out. I forced a smile. "I have some reading to do, anyway."

LAILA

I **poured her** a full glass of chianti.
Recognizing my same doubts in her saddened me. I knew all too well its consuming force. That sense of no control. When the world spins and you can't stop it. You drown in your own anxiety, and are only tugged deeper below the waves.

"Here," I said. "For your nerves."

She took the goblet and swallowed a large swig.

"I might need the entire jug," she jested.

I chuckled and faced her, sitting down on the pillows by the fire.

"People love to tell you not to fear, but you can't just stop. It's uncontrollable," I said. She nodded. "But that doesn't mean you can't push forward. You are spiraling, but the trick is to pretend and carry on. It's damn hard, but possible."

I touched her shoulder, and she sighed.

"I appreciate Tristan trying to give me confidence. He is a great strength, but he wasn't there. He doesn't understand what I did, and quite frankly, neither do you." She shrugged me off. "I'm tired of people trying to relate. Of people telling me I'm courageous, when I welcomed and rejoiced in the power that took me over that day."

My thoughts returned to that dungeon so many years ago, and to the stranger who offered me a kingdom in exchange for my child. And I accepted. Gleefully.

"Tell me, then," I said. "Help me understand."

She stared into the fire.

"There was a spinning wheel," she whispered. "Beautiful, how the wood curved and glowed in the candle light. It almost shone like..."

"Gold," I finished, not meaning too.

She raised an eyebrow.

"Yes, gold. I never questioned its existence. I only knew it wanted me. I wanted it. A voice told me not to touch the spindle, that I should resist for the sake of my family, and my kingdom." She took another drink of wine. "I wanted to heed the voice, but these women. They dazzled me with their ethereal grace. They told me the spinning wheel was my destiny."

I swallowed hard. She obviously spoke of Clotho and Lachesis.

"Then, the spindle," she continued. "It glinted so prettily. How could something so beautiful be so dangerous?"

The image of Rumpelstiltskin strengthened in my mind. He sat at the spinning wheel, the golden thread whipping around the bobbin as he treadled. It glinted through his fingers as it pulled and twisted. He was beautiful. The entire thing was beautiful.

"The voice told me not to touch the spindle. My heart told me not to touch the spindle, but as the women led me towards the machine, my soul told me to give in. To press my finger into the sharpened point and give it my blood. It wanted to taste me. To have me. And I chose to give it all I was."

My own finger burned where my blood spilled onto Rumpelstiltskin's contract. When I had given him all *I* was.

"I know the sensation exactly," I said, without thought.

"You don't," she replied, her words hard. "You know nothing of such things."

I stood and walked to the window. Stars flickered in the inky black.

"You have no idea what I know," I whispered. "You are not the only one that gave into such temptation. That let the soul lead when the heart, when reason, said no."

Rustling fabric moved behind me. Rose approached.

"You mean you also have experience with magic and spinning wheels? You mock me."

"I don't mock you."

I turned and faced her. Confusion riddled her expression.

"What are you saying?"

The words caught in the back of my throat. I never told anyone about it all before.

"There was a...man," I pushed out, my throat tight and raw. "Or, a being. I'm still not sure. But he came to me when my life was threatened."

She gripped my arms and led me to the settee. We sat and I twisted my skirts in my hands.

"It's ok, you can tell me," she said.

"Years ago, before Tristan was born, I was ordered to spin straw into gold, or face death. I could not do such a thing, and feared for my life." I paused, taking a breath. "This man, this stranger, offered me an escape, but at a terrible price. I accepted, though it was wrong. I gave into my selfishness. But that whirr of the spinning wheel, that music rising from its turning gears enraptured me, rendering me a monster."

My eyes burned. I cleared my throat, not finished.

"Exactly as you, I harmed those I loved. But we can't be bound to our past sins. Failure doesn't decide who we are. It doesn't determine where we can go. I was once told pain is power. Harness your pain, let it become your power to overcome."

She nodded, and embraced me.

"I'm sorry for my harshness, earlier. I never would believe..."

"No one would," I interrupted. "It's quite alright."

"Thank you for sharing. I feel lighter, like the darkness has lifted."

We parted, and I held her gaze.

"That's what I hoped."

I rose and poured chianti to the brim of my own goblet. I needed something to banish the ghosts of my own past I summoned. I lifted the wine to my lips, and took a large sip.

"The man you spoke of, is that Rumpelstiltskin?"

Chianti spilled over my knuckles and splattered on the oak floorboards.

"Whatever made you think of that?"

I placed the goblet on a side table, and fell to my knees, dabbing up the spilled wine with my kerchief. Rose came to my side, helping to soak up the crimson with a tattered cloth.

"How he looks at you. The storms in his eyes, they rage only for you. The same that are in your own for him. I'm not a fool. Something happened between you both in the past."

I stopped wiping the floor, frozen. My throat tightened, and I sucked in a breath holding back tears.

I nodded. For the first time admitting the truth.

"Yes."

I wiped the stain again, pressing hard into the wood.

"Do you love him?"

I rubbed faster, hoping she would stop her inquiry, but secretly hoping to speak more of what weighed so long on my heart.

"It's complicated," I said.

"It's a simple question."

I threw the kerchief down and stood, crossing my arms across my chest.

Simple? She knew nothing. Bitterness washed through me.

"You have a simple notion of love. To you love is innocence and flowers. Sweet nothings whispered in ears on summer days. Promises made that are kind and good."

I sat back on the settee, pressing my head into my hands. She sat beside me.

"Love is love," she said.

I chuckled darkly. If only she knew.

"Not ours. Our love is dirty. Disgusting. It was born of dark and twisted things. It's why our love can never be, or should have ever been."

"That's not true," she said. "Love is good. Pure. Darkness might have brought you together, but the goodness in you bore love and that love is salvation. You need to take it. Cherish it. Nourish it. Let love wash away the sins you feel you have committed. Pain might be power, but love is strength."

"I...can't..."

She wrapped me in her arms and rocked me, giving me comfort as if my own mother.

"I don't try to be cruel, Laila. I've seen both your suffering, and it makes me weep. Two souls that have found love in the other should not remain apart. You've helped me, and now I must return the favor."

Her words undid me.

Utterly.

I buried my face in her shoulder and wept. I never cried such bitter tears.

"I'm only complete when I'm with him," I sobbed. I didn't realize how much I needed someone to listen, to know. "I do love him. I love him with my every breath."

I shocked myself how openly I admitted what I never wanted to voice. Pulling back, I wiped the wet from my eyes. She took my hands and squeezed. I sucked back the tears that threatened to come again.

"That's significant," she said. "Go to him, and tell him. Light always chases away the darkness."

❦

THE WALLS OF OUR ROOM PRESSED AGAINST ME. I HAD TO LEAVE.

Walking across the cobblestones I relished in the silent night air. In the swiftness and monotony of my every step. I walked through all the words Rose told me. Walked through my hopes and my dreams and my fears. My guilt.

With no knowledge how I ended up there, I pulled on a cold iron handle of a church door.

Incense hung thick around the pillars. Stone blackened from centuries of candle smoke rose high over my head as I passed pews of heavy mahogany.

I approached the warm glow of candles on a side altar. Saints of fading blues, lilacs, and pinks stood on carved filigrees above me. Dropping a copper coin into the metal box, I took a thin beeswax candle and lit the wick. I stuck it among the other tilted flames in the sand.

I fell to my knees, the chill of the stone seeping into my kneecaps.

Lacing my fingers together, I pressed my hands against my chin. Quiet surrounded me. A peaceful reverence I longed for and breathed in, deeply.

"Can I love him?" I asked the still.

No reply came.

I closed my eyes, breathing in again. Smoke and incense filled my lungs. My memories rose like ghosts.

Fire surrounded Rumpelstiltskin. Flames. Chaos. He rose from the water after risking his life for me.

I pushed my hands closer together. *Can I love him?*

My mind shot forward. He stood before Fate now, and offered him his soul in exchange for me and Tristan.

You don't know what I'd give to repay the pain I've caused you. Just to have your forgiveness, he had told me that night we shared. That night I'd never forget.

When I was with him, when he moved within me, I never felt so complete. So whole. We became one in our love. But in the light of day, I couldn't accept it. Shame doused me in what we had done.

I wanted my love for him to wither. It only strengthened. It knit into every stitch of my heart and my soul until my entire being thrived on my love for this man.

Though born out of the black, the love we shared made us both better people. But did that make it right?

I opened my eyes, letting my hands fall to my sides.

The fading saint wore a serene smile. I understood, then.

CHAPTER EIGHT

RUMPELSTILTSKIN

W   *ithin you lies the key*, the Oracle's voice whispered in my memory. *Allow it to guide your way.*
  Those words haunted me, angered me, because they held possibility. Possibility I kept ignoring, because the truth was too grim to contemplate.

Laila held hope of discovering the mystery of Fate's sisters in some book. Futile. When Rose couldn't help us, I knew I couldn't avoid what I feared anymore.

The key to finding Clotho and Lachesis was within me.

The growing, searing agony ripping through my hand proved it. It bore into my bones now, gnawed into my raw flesh, and filled my core with terror.

I suspected as much for a long time. Since I met that accursed Oracle in the woods. At first I shrugged off her words as soothsaying nonsense. But as we kept failing, and my scar dredged into my sinew tethering me more to Fate, I realized it might not be metaphor, but fact.

Only one way to find out loomed before me. The others believed I sought Darius for ancient knowledge. If it could only be so simple.

I shuddered.

I entered an abandoned church. Dust hung in the air, and I brushed cobwebs away as I approached the altar. Burial stones took up large sections of the marble floor. Gripping an iron handle I pulled, my arms straining to lift the slab. The metal scratched and disintegrated within my palm.

The stone rose and I pushed, scraping it across the grit and dirt. A dark shoot vanished into black. Sweat broke out on my forehead, and I wiped it away. Throwing my legs over the sides, I slid down into the crypt.

I landed on my backside, cold earth and wood shavings breaking my fall. I pressed into the ground and lifted myself, brushing the dust off my elbows and kneecaps.

Twisting my wrist, a flame ignited in my palm, illuminating a room of death. Coffins lined the edges in tidy rows, with a larger row down the middle. Deep yellow paint covered the coffins, symbols of religion and hourglasses fading from decay.

I pressed on.

Skulls placed within walls of bone and fragments grinned at me as I passed.

I tried not to think about the breath on the back of my neck. I turned. No one. Only shadows that loomed and towered behind me.

"The haunting chill is quite invigorating, is it not?" a voice asked. "I love how it enlivens the blood."

He smelled the crook of my neck. I hated how panic vibrated my veins from his games.

"You always love making an entrance," I said.

"One must have vices to endure eternity," he said. "Once you reach your second or third millennium, you will find the same."

I faced Darius, finding him exactly as I remembered. Points and shadows and soft black curls fell over hard eyes. His poreless skin made him appear as bronzed marble. Everything about him breathed with ancient grace.

"Does eternity also drive you underground? I knew you were a corpse, but never imagined you'd live like one."

He narrowed his gaze, and his eyes flashed in vivid blue.

"I prefer the silence. Besides, it makes it much easier to dispose of my meals," he said. "Though I may be a dead thing, I do not live like one."

He walked away, motioning to follow him. He moved like a whisper, making me feel like a clumsy giant.

We entered through a side door and into a lush room. Firelight danced across tapestries, and Persian rugs covered the inlaid floor. Color, luxury, and vibrancy overwhelmed me.

He lifted a crystal decanter and poured a glass of whiskey.

"I didn't know vampires drank whiskey," I said.

"We don't," he replied. "But I enjoy the scent of peat moss and the memories."

"I never pegged you as sentimental."

"Two thousand years will do that to you," he replied.

He swirled it twice, then closed his eyes as he inhaled. He offered me nothing. The message was clear.

Silence.

"Darius, I—"

He threw his glass into the flames and they roared making his beauty terrifying. I shivered. I expected his rage, but it didn't make it any more palatable.

"You threaten and torture my servant, you break into my home uninvited. Did you expect we would actually share some whiskey like old friends when you barge in here with that *thing* on your hand?" He pointed to the scar on my palm. The proof of my deal with Fate.

"I didn't expect anything but a chance to be heard," I said.

"I do not appreciate you blazing into my life like this. You promised me we would never cross paths again after that horror with the girl in the dungeon. You just couldn't listen. I see things haven't changed. That wound grows even deeper."

Darius made it his mission to keep track of any with magical gifts. He found me when I first awoke to my new world of magic and revenge. He became a kind of mentor.

But when he discovered how I came by my magic, that Fate marked me as his, he made me promise I wouldn't let my revenge darken me further. I didn't listen, of course. Edward's demise was far too delicious a treat to turn away from.

After that, he forbade me to see him again. He wanted no part in the infection I carried. I vowed to obey, but here I stood, brazenly disobedient. The only deal I ever broke.

"I've grown since we parted. I've changed," I said.

He scoffed.

"Men like you don't change, especially ones that make deals with demons. It's why I couldn't harbor you anymore. I wanted no responsibility for your vile, base enterprises."

"I don't need to be scolded like a child."

"Then stop behaving so reckless. I know of your current plight, and the stakes you face. I have eyes and ears everywhere."

I sighed. I stepped towards him, he took one back.

"Then you must know what I want. What I need you to do. Help me."

He shook his head.

"While I hate Fate to my core, he has no power over me anymore. Since I died a man and rose a vampire, I freed myself from his chains. I have no wish to cross him. Unlike you, he keeps his bargains."

That hurt.

"What about for humanity's sake?"

"I can feed on them whether they have destiny or not."

My mouth fell open. He claimed I was heartless, when here he stood, able to help and remaining disastrously neutral.

"You really have no care for them? I thought you respected their lives."

He laughed, and the room filled with thunder.

"Are you saying you do? I've watched you manipulate, take, steal, and cheat. Don't pretend to start caring now."

I paused.

"You're right. But I do care for my son, and for his mother."

It still seemed a weird thing to refer to Tristan as my son, but he truly was mine. I would fight for him until my last breath.

Darius' eyes lit with curiosity.

"What's this? Does the beast have a heart after all?"

If only he knew how my heart pounded for Laila and Tristan. What

I'd given, and what I would still give. They were my very life, and I would not surrender. I would not fail them. He had to understand.

"The world can burn, but not them. I will do anything to save Laila and Tristan. Darius, I ask you a small thing. Help me, and I will never bother you again."

"If you haven't noticed, your promises hold little weight."

I fell to my knees and looked up at him. The man Darius last saw would never grovel at his feet. I hoped he might change his mind if he saw my actions match my words.

"Please."

His mouth parted staring down at me. His brow furrowed, as if thinking.

"You ask me to do this because of love?"

"Yes," I replied. "I know what I have been in the past. What I have done. But now, I only want to spare two innocent souls the punishment of my sins."

Silence.

He neared me and lifted me back to my feet. His finger chilled me as he placed it between my neck and my collar, pulling the stiff fabric down. He touched the vein in my neck, and I felt my pulse throb against his knuckles.

"It will be dangerous. I might not be able to stop."

He removed his hand and I swallowed down a dry lump.

"The oracle told me the key to all the answers I seek is within me. I'm hoping if it can be shown, then we have a fighting chance to find Clotho and Lachesis. That we can end Fate's plans, and right all the wrongs I've committed because of my stupidity. My selfishness."

His eyes lightened.

"While I applaud your gaining somewhat of a conscience, I still don't like this."

"Only a vampire has the powers to discern what lurks within the soul. Only you can tell me what key the Oracle said hides inside me. It's our only hope to end Fate's plans."

"Yes, but—"

"You told me to turn from Fate, and I didn't listen. I'm sorry I disobeyed you. Now, I'm here, asking your forgiveness. Asking help to rid him from me. Rid him from harming others."

He took in a large breath. Going back to his decanter, he filled a clean glass with whiskey. I expected him to lift it to his nose again, but instead he handed it to me.

"I would drink if I were you. To dull the excruciating agony," he whispered.

"You'll do it?"

He leaned into me, breathing in, as if wanting to be enveloped in my scent.

"I've never tasted one like you." Hunger lit in his eyes. "A fellow immortal. This will be an experience for both of us."

My throat went dry.

"Drink, before I change my mind," he said.

I shot it back, the alcohol burning my throat down to my stomach. As the last drop slipped over the edge of the glass, he gripped my shoulder with one hand, and dug into my jaw with the other. He pressed, forcing my neck to lengthen, revealing my exposed flesh to him.

"Vulnerable, and delicate, the neck," he whispered, his lips moving over my skin.

His fangs sank into me. Pain exploded through my muscle and tendons. He locked his lips against my throat and drank, pulling me into him. My fingers and toes grew cold. My heat, my life, surged up through my heart and into his suckling mouth.

The world spun and the agony sparked with bites of pleasure. Torment gave way to euphoria. Sound and color enveloped me. I no longer cared about the damp chill in my arms and legs. I no longer cared how my heartbeat slowed in my ears.

In fact, it ceased beating all together. Tranquility embraced me. Darkness. Beautiful, beautiful darkness.

Arms lifted me and sat me on a chaise. Red wine passed my lips and slipped down my throat. Warmth returned to my fingers, and my heart gained strength.

Darius stared at me, his lips stained crimson with my blood. That wasn't what chilled me. It was his eyes.

Hollow, and terrified.

"What have you done?" he asked.

My head throbbed and it was hard to concentrate on his words.

"Done?"

He lifted the wine to my lips again. The world started to sharpen.

"I've never experienced anything like it, before," he said. "Your soul is not fully yours."

"What do you mean it isn't fully mine?" My words wanted to slur.

"It's linked with something dark. A shade."

My throat went dry. I didn't want to think about what that meant. Only one thing filled my thoughts.

"Did you see the key? Tell me."

He got up and stared at the fire. He rubbed my blood from his lips onto his silk sleeve.

"I couldn't," he said. "I was prevented."

Ice rolled down my spine. I tried to stand, but fell back into the satin cushion.

"You must have some idea. Surely you saw something."

He shook his head.

"I could only sense a secret beneath the waves, but it remained shrouded. *It* didn't want me to see."

"It?"

"A shadow."

A deep, and sickening chill rolled through my gut.

A shadow! Mina echoed in my memory. The Pythin sister's screams filled my mind. *You boy, are destined for a dual spirit.*

Your journey is hidden among shadows, the Oracle echoed.

"No..." I whispered.

He laid a hand on my shoulder.

"I'm sorry. I wish you well with your quest, but I can offer you no more help."

I pushed him off me. Anger took over my despair.

"That's it then?" I spat, overwhelmed. "Damn you, damn it all!"

"Don't get angry at me, I've done what you asked."

I paced, trying to breathe even breaths. I tried to keep my resolve, my strength, though all I wanted to do was fall to the ground and cry. I failed, and my hope dwindled to a single ember.

My palm scalded in burning agony. Fate laughed at me.

Darius neared me, and held my face to his. He looked into my eyes, as if inspecting me like some race horse.

"You look like shit," he said, pushing me back. "I suspect you never sleep, do you?"

"I have no need of sleep," I said.

He nodded, placing his finger below his nose.

"If I can offer you advice, I suggest you sleep. Sometimes things open to us when we allow the mind to rest. You might be surprised."

I didn't care for his advice. I couldn't concentrate on his words anymore.

I thought only of the shadow clinging to my soul. It blocked the key I needed, blocked any chance at our succeeding. But what was it?

My scar smoldered and I feared we would never win.

LAILA

I **waited alone** in Rumpelstiltskin's room for him to return. I couldn't wait a minute more to tell him what weighed on my heart.

I sat at a heavy oak table, twisting scraps of parchment before tearing them to little bits. It kept me from insanity as my heart pounded in my throat. My mind raced with what I would tell him. How did one even start such conversations? A cacophony of "forgive me's" and "I love you's" repeated and repeated until I thought my head would burst.

But what if he changed his mind?

I tore the corners off my mangled paper, letting them drop to the rough wood along with my anxiety.

The door opened and I lifted my gaze. Rumpelstiltskin walked in, not noticing me sitting in the shadows. He threw his cloak on the bed and sank into the duvet, staring at his feet.

I stood, my blood rushing in my ears. Sweat beaded on my back. Lightheadedness caused me to believe I stood in a dream. I swallowed down my nerves, and kept reminding myself to breathe.

"Rumpelstiltskin..." I pushed out. He looked up, and concern riddled his face.

I dared a step forward. He rose from his bed, but remained in place, as if timid to approach me.

"What's wrong? Are you well?" he asked.

My cheeks burned.

"Quite well."

His shoulders relaxed.

"Good."

Our eyes remained locked together as silence swelled. He scratched behind his ear, then cleared his throat.

"Is there another reason you've come, then? I thought you didn't want to be around me."

"I didn't." Confusion twisted his eyebrows. "But—"

My words caught in the back of my throat. All the things I wanted to tell him vanished, only my thundering heart remaining. He needed to know I loved him and was wrong to ever deny it. He needed to know I would be his. And dammit, in that moment I needed my voice most, I became a mute fool.

I neared him, wanting to take his hands and kiss them. If I couldn't tell him, then I could at least show him how I felt.

I stopped. Cold chilled my veins.

Blood. Blood crusted on the side of his neck, staining his white shirt poking out of his doublet. Red fingerprints marked his jaw and right cheek.

"Your throat!" I exclaimed. "Sit down and let me look."

He clapped his hand over the wound, as if embarrassed.

"It's nothing."

"That's more than nothing," I replied. "There's a gaping wound torn in your skin."

I pulled out a chair and motioned him to sit. He grumbled, but obeyed, the chair groaning beneath his weight.

I placed a kettle of water over the flames to boil.

"I'm not used to such injury," he said, wincing. "Usually wounds heal instantly on me, but when it is inflicted by a fellow immortal. Well, you can plainly see."

I shook my head as I tore clean cloth into bandages.

"Why did he do this?" I asked

He remained silent for a second or two.

"Because I asked him too."

"Of all the madness! I thought you went to discuss Clotho and Lachesis, not willingly go as a meal."

He lowered his head, and gazed into the fire.

"I couldn't tell you the truth. You would never have let me go."

He was right.

"Why? Why was such violence necessary?"

He sighed and pushed back in his chair, straightening his spine.

"Only vampires can see inside another's soul. The Oracle told me the key to everything rests inside me. I asked Darius to drink my blood so I might know what this key actually is. I thought it would be the missing piece we needed to end Fate."

I shuddered. This man was wholly brave, and wholly stupid.

"I can't believe you did that alone. You should have let me come with you."

His gaze shot to mine, fervor glinting in his irises.

"And risk your life? No, never again."

Silence.

"Did Darius see what you wanted?"

He leaned forward again, and pushed his head in his hands.

"He saw nothing. Only a shadow."

"Shadow?"

"Something lives in me, Laila," his voice cracked. "Some dark force. The Oracle saw this shade, those sisters I lived with threw me out because of it. Darius...he could only tell me my soul is not my own. Whatever key the Oracle spoke of is unable to be revealed because the shadow won't allow it. I don't think...I don't think we will win. That was my last ace."

He sucked in a deep breath, staccatos of emotion causing it to flutter.

I slowly reached out and touched his knee, to remind him he wasn't alone. He lifted his head and stared at my hand as I squeezed. Red misted the whites of his eyes.

"We will find another way," I said, though I wasn't really sure one existed.

He smirked and sat back.

"Your optimism does you credit, but it doesn't erase the fact I failed you. I failed everyone."

I didn't like his black mood. I couldn't let him fall away into doubt and hopelessness. This wasn't over until it was over.

The kettle roared as the water boiled. I took it off the fire and poured it into a porcelain bowl.

"Remove your shirt," I said.

He tensed, and bit his lip. My heart raced, somehow finding his nervousness endearing.

"I don't think that's necessary," he said.

"Now's not the time to be shy. Your neck looks horrid. At least let me clean you up."

He shrugged.

"It's not that bad."

I put my hands at my hips and tapped my foot, staring him down. He sighed, and gave in.

His fingers worked his buttons, slipping them through the narrow slits with effortless grace. His white linen shirt hung half open, and I couldn't help admiring his lean muscle.

I'd never seen him without his stiff clothes. True, I had felt his naked body against mine, but the night shrouded us in darkness. Now, I wanted to reach out and trace his firm chest, following the hard ridges down his stomach.

I tried to keep steady as heat flushed between my legs.

He tried to pull his arm through his sleeve, cringing as he cried out from pain.

I aided him, peeling away the blood soaked collar from his neck. Lifting his shirt over his head, my fingers brushed his hot skin. He shuddered beneath me.

Another throb of heat rushed to my toes. He cleared his throat and shifted in his chair.

The air thickened around us.

I took a breath. Then a second.

Grabbing one of the cloths, I dipped it into the scalding water. I forced myself to hold in a sob as I stared at his injury. The pain he must suffer astounded me.

Bite marks punctured deep into his skin. Flesh and gore streamed down to his collarbone. The vampire hadn't just sank his teeth into him, he had chewed and tore. My stomach pitted and I cursed Darius.

I wiped the wounds gently, hating how he hissed as I caused him more agony. I pulled the cloth across the skin, cleaning the blood, cleaning the mangled flesh. As I worked, the marks shrank, no doubt his magic slowly repairing his injury. Confidence filled me that in a day or two, he would be back to normal.

I wrapped bandages around his shoulder, crossing his chest, and around his back. He trembled again as I grazed his skin. I hoped he didn't notice my pounding heart.

"There," I said, tying the bandage tight.

He inspected my work, giving a nod of approval.

"Thank you," he replied.

He glowed in the firelight. As he had when he spun the straw into gold for me. My pulse had quickened for him then, and it quickened for him now.

I reached out and pressed my hand against his chest. His heart pounded into my palm. Heat flushed my cheeks.

His pupils dilated, and a deep hunger rippled through me, hard and wicked. I wanted to taste him again. I quivered finally outlining the sculpted lines of his chest, trailing down to his stomach. Then lower.

He grasped my wrist and pulled me onto his lap, having me straddle him. His desire pressed against me. I lost myself in the scent of woodsmoke and cedar rising from his skin.

Want roared through me. I claimed his lips, and his passion matched my own. We kissed deeply, our tongues exploring the other. My blood ignited as he rocked his hips, obliterating the world outside of us.

I broke the kiss, my lips throbbing with blood. I loved the need darkening his expression. He kissed the exposed length of my neck intensely, devouring every inch of my skin, and I thought I would lose my wits.

Frenzy took us over, our base, animal lusts rising to the surface.

"I shouldn't love you," I gasped, digging my nails into his back as pleasure pulsed in my core. "I don't want to love you, but I can't stop. I never will."

He coiled his fingers in my hair, the bites of pain adding to the thrill tightening deep within me.

"You think I feel any different?" he asked, trailing his hand up my leg. "Since I first saw you in those hills of straw, I've burned for you."

Our mouths locked again, our lips moving as fast as our beating hearts. I drowned in his taste, and I craved more. I flicked open the buttons of his trousers, taking him in my hand.

He pushed me away, as if I woke him from a dream.

"No," he said, his words rough and breathless. "I...can't. I can't do this to you."

Confusion rippled within me, bordering on hurt. After all this, did he not want me? He had to be joking.

I crossed my arms.

"Are you serious?"

He nodded, biting his lip.

"Please, understand."

Anger replaced my confusion.

"Understand what, exactly? I offer you my love, and you turn me away."

"Laila..."

"You said you burned for me."

"You have no idea how much. There's nothing more I want than your heart. Then to take you right now on the bed and be yours."

"If that's true, what's stopping you?"

An emotion greater than sadness overcame him. He withered into a broken thing, and I didn't know how to repair him. My rage cooled.

"You need to let me go," he whispered.

"What madness are you speaking about?"

He turned away, leaning over the heavy table.

"The truth is I never was yours, Laila. I've only ever been Fate's. Since the beginning, I was only his. He's won."

My blood ran cold. I didn't like these words. I didn't like what these thoughts made him become.

"Stop this."

"Can't you see?" He turned and lifted his hand, holding out his scar to me. His debt to Fate. "He owns me. I will never be free of him. Now I've failed, I must accept my place as his toy."

He was always careful not to let me see his scar, and now I knew why. A crevice of marred and sinewy flesh almost cut through to the other side of his hand. It was far deeper than I recalled, as if the debt slowly ate him.

"You are mine, not his," I said.

He tried to smile, but he couldn't. Red misted his eyes again.

"We will continue as planned to the portal back to Dream tomorrow. We will give him Rose, fulfilling my bargain. You will get your soul returned, and Tristan will keep his life. That poor girl...she was damned from the start."

I couldn't bear the thought of Rose falling into the darkness of Fate's wicked plans.

"We can't stop fighting," I said. The words seemed stupid to me now, as acceptance of the truth started to gnaw at my resolve. But admitting our failure I still could not do. Not when time remained.

"I made the deal I did for your freedom, and I'd do it again. All of it. But I can't have you loving a ghost. I'm sorry, Laila. I found you only to lose you again."

I shook my head. I hated Fate more than I knew possible. He made the man I love crumble, and worse, bereft of hope.

"No," I said.

"But—"

"I love you," I interjected. "You once said you will never stop fighting for me. I will never stop fighting for you. And *if* these are our final moments before the end, I want to spend them in your arms."

I took his scarred hand and uncurled his fingers. I traced the jagged edges of his wound, the thing he deepened when he took Fate's deal to save my life.

"You are a part of me, and I you. Not gods or beasts will keep us separated any longer."

I lifted his hand to my lips and kissed his scar, loving him. He shook beneath my touch. I held his gaze, and disbelief glinted in his eyes.

"I'm so afraid," he whispered.

I laced my fingers with his, and squeezed.

"I will be with you until the end."

I wrapped my arms around him and claimed his mouth. He melted into my embrace.

Everything we ever were lived in that kiss. Pain, lust, power, love... My body sang as desire tore through my depths. My legs shook as heat throbbed between them again.

We fell onto the duvet. His fingers made quick work tearing into my laces, releasing my breasts. He took me into his mouth, and pleasure crashed over me.

I moaned, digging into his scalp, pressing him against me. I loved the sensation of his lips on my breast. I tugged at his trousers, while he ran his hand up my skirts, lifting them around my waist.

His muscles flexed as he straddled me, kissing me deeply. I savored his taste, drowning in him as his hand found me.

Molten lava burned in my core, tightening around him as he moved his fingers slowly. Agonizingly slowly. I gasped as waves washed me in bliss.

My skin sizzled as I ran down his ridges, towards his hips letting him know I needed him. Now.

I wanted to remember every inch of him. I wanted to burn his scent into my memory. Incase we never held each other again, at least we would have this night.

He skated his lips down my neck as he entered me, filling me completely. I cried out as my body shuddered in delight. I lost myself as he moved in me. Gentle strokes at first, as if he savored my body around his.

I dug my heels into his legs as our hips moved together. I clawed at his back, and he moved faster. Our rhythm doused me in euphoria.

Still, I needed more.

I turned him on his back, rocking him into me. His eyes were black and hungry. He ground his teeth, and his gasps filled my ears over the thunder of my heart.

I gripped into his chest, and he dug into my hips. We crashed together as our pace quickened, and I wasn't sure how much longer we would both last.

I pressed him harder into me, holding his arms as I soared towards the edge.

Ecstasy. Cascading intoxication.

I whimpered as I lost myself to him, never wanting to be found again. He fell next. Delirium took us both, engulfing us in pleasure.

In that moment the monsters at our door did not exist. We were free, and nothing could catch us.

CHAPTER NINE

Skirting:

Verb: Removal of debris and waste wool from fleece

Verb: Attempt to ignore; avoid dealing with (to avoid especially because of difficulty of fear of controversy)

TRISTAN

My father's diary laid on the table, still unopened.

Sweat beaded on my palms as I tapped my leg. Everything I wanted to know lay inside, and that terrified me.

Sucking in a breath, I picked up the book. The leather crumbled beneath my fingers, and the binding cracked as I opened the cover. My father's neat and curled letters filled the page. I smiled at how similar our hands looked, though my loops weren't so large.

My heart ached. The letters disintegrated into Pater's face as he filled my thoughts. There would be no returning once I read the contents. All my memories of him might be forever tarnished.

I became five years old again, sitting on Pater's knee as he told me dark tales. Then I was older, and he taught me how to fight with swords, praising my parries. Then I was me now, and he sacrificed his soul to help protect my life.

I tried to push him away, wanting to concentrate only on my real father's words.

My mother entered my mind, now. Pride filled her expression. She told me I was a good man, and that she loved me. I loved her.

My palms started to sweat again. Did I really want the truth about them both?

I traced my thumb over my father's writing, unsure what to do.

The spine pressed into my hand and I chilled. It had once pressed into my father's hand the same way. This diary connected me to him. To his memories, his intimate thoughts. To a ghost I always wanted to know.

And now, I didn't know if I could let him speak.

He was a great man, a great friend, and a better king. Until he came..., Lord Hochstein's voice echoed concerning my true father, and the other man who raised me as his son.

Decision flared in me. Speculation ended now. It wasn't fair to keep my father silent because of my fear.

The pages threatened to disintegrate as I turned them gently. A heavy scent of mildew rose into my nose.

My heart thundered in my ears as I read.

March 7

Went hunting for stags, but the animals kept disappearing into the thicket.

Discovered a shivering creature hiding in the frosted leaves. A small dog, gray and wire haired. I picked him up and he kissed my beard. His thin skin and protruding bones concerned me. I would not have him suffer anymore.

Riding back to the castle I held him against me beneath my furs to keep him warm. Once back in my rooms, he yipped and wagged his tale as I caressed him. The servants brought hot water and I bathed him myself. He kept licking me, and his tale beat against my arms. The joy of this simple creature warmed my heart.

I made sure he dined on beef that night. Now he sleeps on silk by my bed.

The story warmed my heart. A patron of lost animals. I imagined the entire story in my mind. The little gray dog, and my father running his fingers through his thick fur.

I read on, enjoying more of his tales. Of his jabs and remarks on friends and stuffy advisors. His intricate views on politics and religion.

May 4

A peasant girl has been discovered with the power to spin straw into gold.

I didn't believe it at first. I am continually lied to and my kindness taken advantage of. But, I gave her the benefit of the doubt, and provided her the chance to test her abilities.

When I walked into a room filled with towers and bobbins filled with golden thread, I knew God had blessed me.

She will be the key to securing our kingdom's strength. We will remain a beacon of power and knowledge.

Laila is a beautiful creature in her own right. I am making her my queen, as there can be no better woman, or dowry.

Blood rushed in my ears, and my breaths shortened. I pulled my finger over my mother's name.

Spinning straw into gold? She never mentioned such an odd ability.

I tore through page after page, searching for more mention of my mother. His entries grew less frequent, and if they did appear, it concerned calculations of the gold he now acquired. Of exotic silks he purchased.

Then, a mention of how my mother's beauty intensified as her stomach swelled with his heir. A prize he said was above all others.

My throat went dry. He spoke of me.

February 18

I am a father.

Laila delivered me a healthy son this day. Prince Tristan, the jewel of my eye. I never knew my love could be so great. He will make a formidable king one day, and secure our family line. My lineage is now safe, and the crown protected.

Tristan is my love, and my security.

I stroked the word "love," almost hearing my father breathe the word to me through the fading ink.

I continued on. There were more entries about me. Dozens! Each day he wrote about my progress. If I cried, if I laughed, or if I slept soundly in his arms.

My eyes burned, and I blinked away the tears that threatened to fall. I always wondered what he thought of me. If I made him happy, or if he loved me. In his own words, I finally knew the answers to all my questions.

Pride at being his son and heir swelled in my heart. It pulsed through my veins and solidified who I was.

A prince.

I feared breaking the journal as I read with voracious speed. His tone remained lifted and calm, until the beginning of March.

March 3

The devil came today.

A man of black hair and sickly complexion. He looks familiar, but I can't place the face.

He claimed Laila owes him a debt. That she owes him my son.

She tricked me with her tales of spinning straw into gold. The truth is this creature spun the gold for her. She traded my beautiful son to him in exchange for upholding her ruse. In exchange of becoming queen.

Clearly the woman is his whore.

I threatened the imp. I would not allow my child taken from me.

He offered a new bargain. I have three days to learn his name, and if I do, Tristan remains safe in my arms. I swear he will remain mine regardless.

No creature will separate father from son.

Cold sweat drenched my back, and I trembled as I flipped to the next page. The final entry.

March 10

His name is Rumpelstiltskin.

I've won.

The journal fell from my grip and clapped against the floorboards. Sickness twisted my stomach and I thought I would heave.

Your father's blood stains his hands

Lord Hochstein was right. It was true. All of it.

I wiped clammy sweat off my forehead. Sounds grew loud and distant. A vortex of hatred, bitterness, and betrayal threatened to sweep me off my feet.

I sat in a chair and pressed my face in my hands, letting it sink in.

They murdered my father. Together, they murdered him.

All this time, I believed Fate was the enemy. That Fate killed my father, and took my crown, but now I saw the truth. My hatred was focused on the wrong creature.

The thought of Pater, *Rumpelstiltskin*, whatever he was, brought bile up my throat. It burned, but not as strong as the inferno of rage in my chest. What kind of sick thing was he to ask for a child? To take my father's life?

And my mother...what mother gives up a child to a demon for her own gain? She lied to me from the start. She told me she loved me.

How could she love someone she forsook at their most vulnerable and innocent?

She was a fraud. They both were.

And they lied to me. Deceived me in every way a person could be deceived.

I jumped up and ran to the porcelain basin and stuck my head inside, retching. The truth cracked my core, grinding it into grit.

It all made sense now.

True he had read to me stories as a child, but it turned to cold resentment. As I grew, he praised my swordsmanship, but he then disappeared for months at a time. He shut me out, kept me prisoner, until now when he finally had use of me.

And mother. She stuffed me with sweets to hide her bitter heart. She told me she loved me, only to distract me so I wouldn't see her tears that her bargain with the creature had failed. I hated her.

They both made me a fool.

Wiping the vomit from my lips, I bent down and picked up the diary. A letter slipped out from between the pages. It was addressed to me.

My heart continued to pound, and blood rushed through my head.

Lord Hochstein's signature shone like a beacon as I broke open the seal.

Your Royal Highness,

If you are reading this letter, then you've finally learned the truth I warned you about.

You and your companion are unsafe in your current company. They only seek their own power.

Whatever quest they say you are on, is a lie. They only wish your destruction.

You are the true heir to the kingdom. As this diary proves, your father loved you, and wanted nothing more than for you to rule.

I pledge to you my protection. Come to me at Schloss Hofbrunn. Together, we will win back your crown and have these vile usurpers punished for the murder of your dear father.

They will taste the pain of justice.

Your humble servant, and loving godfather,

Lord Hochstein

I had to get Rose to safety. Now.

These were villains that only sought power, and they used honied words to ensnare. Their lies were so deep, so entrenched with rot, I didn't doubt Fate was some grand ploy to trap us both. And it had worked.

We were both heirs, after all. Why take one kingdom, when you could take two?

I shivered at whatever twisted future awaited us if we stayed. Sacrifice, blood, curses? My mind ran wild.

I spilled a pot of ink as I smacked a blank piece of parchment on the table. I dipped my quill into the puddle of black and scribbled a note to Lord Hochstein.

I burnt my fingers as I heated the red wax, dripping it over the letter and sealing it shut.

Grabbing a satchel I stuffed it with a full wineskin, adding leftover bread and half a salami. Heaving it over my shoulder, I let myself into Rose's room.

My heart calmed at her sleeping form. She looked as I first saw her in the castle. Peaceful. Perfect.

I knelt down beside her, resisting the urge to kiss her lips. I touched her shoulder, shaking her gently not wanting to startle her.

Her eyes flashed open.

"Tristan?" She pulled the blankets up, covering her chest.

"There isn't time for explanations. You need to go, now. Your life is in danger."

"What kind of danger?"

"Get up, there's no time."

She stumbled out of the bed, and I threw her a cloak. She wrapped it around her, fastening the silver clasp.

We crept down the stairs, and I prayed the floorboards wouldn't creak or pop. A carriage driver sat outside, smoking a pipe.

"You." I grabbed his pipe and tossed it on the ground. His brow lowered in anger. "I'll give you one gold coin if you take this woman to Lord Hochstein at Schloss Hofbrunn. There will be double this waiting for you once you get there."

His eyes brightened, and he smiled revealing all of his four teeth.

"Yes, sir! Right away, sir!"

He stepped up on the carriage, his reins at the ready.

"I don't understand," Rose said. "You aren't coming with me? What of Laila and Rumpelstiltskin?"

I almost had to bite my tongue to keep her from seeing the anger flare at the mention of their names.

"You must trust me," I said. "Lord Hochstein will keep you protected until I fetch you." I handed her my sealed letter. "Give him this. It explains everything. He is a friend. My godfather, in fact. You can trust him."

She nodded, and wrapped her arms around me and kissed me. Heat flushed my cheeks and I dove my fingers into her hair, pressing her harder against my lips. She tasted like heaven.

She pulled away, and I helped her into the carriage.

"Go man, go!" I yelled at the driver.

He whipped the horses and their hooves pounded into the ground, taking my love to safety.

Dawn streaked the sky. The blood moon of Phlegethon was today, but Rose would not be there to play Rumpelstiltskin and Laila's pawn.

And if Fate truly existed, it would be on my terms.

RUMPELSTITLTSKIN

R ed damask surrounded me. A fire blazed.
I walked across Persian rugs in a large study towards a
decanter of port. My head pounded and I poured myself
a glass.

Where was I?

Laughter. Cheers. Bows pulled down thin strings from a far away
violin.

My heart thrashed, realization cascading over me. Dream. I was
back in Dream, in Fate's study.

The glass tumbled from my grip and shattered at my feet, clear
pebbles exploding.

I ran to the door and pulled on the sculpted handle. It wouldn't
open.

Whispers filled my ears. Longing whispers.

I turned and bounded for the windows. They remained sealed
shut.

The whispers grew into cries. Need rolled through me like an ocean
wave. But from where?

Here, the voices called.

Did the voices came from outside me or from within? The sensation of need, of desperation, intensified. My blood tingled with their pleas for salvation.

Here, the voices echoed again, the word soft like a song.

I spun on my heels and faced a malachite urn. The same that took my breath away the first time I saw it. Beautiful piece, with intricate rune marks carved into the green stone.

Another crash of need enveloped me.

Help us!

I moved closer to the vase, like it was the right thing to do. It shook and vibrated. Light glowed around the lid.

I stretched out my arm to touch the top of the stone, wanting to release whatever called me from inside.

I gripped the top of the lid. Pain. Searing pain cut through my hand, radiating down my fingers. I released the stone, believing myself scalded.

A great price is necessary. Greater than any you've yet paid.

The urn and the red damask disintegrated as my eyes flashed open. I laid in my bed, Laila's arm laying across my naked chest.

I shot up and stared at my palm, blinking hard trying to force my eyes to focus. It wasn't burnt or blistered. It appeared as always.

My breaths came hard and quick.

"What's the matter?" Laila groaned, still half asleep.

"The voices. They needed me," I choked out.

She pressed her elbow into the mattress, raising her head.

"It's probably the wind."

I cleared my throat, trying to calm myself. *None of it was real.*

"I was back in Dream and voices spoke to me. I could feel them needing my aid, but I couldn't help them."

She combed her fingers through my hair and kissed my shoulder.

"Go back to sleep. The lark isn't even awake yet."

"No," I said. "If I do, I'll just go back there. I never usually sleep, and every time I do now, I find myself in that place."

Her brow knit with concern.

"How long has this been going on?"

"I've always had strange dreams since I became what I was. But since I rescued you, they've changed. They're vivid, and always the same. I'm in Fate's study, surrounded by garish red damask, Persian rugs, and an urn."

She leaned back in the bed, and pressed her finger below her nose. "What kind of urn?"

"Malachite. Heavy, and decorated in runes. That's where the voices come from. But every time I near it, or touch it, I wake."

She peeled the sheets away, and fumbled in the dim light across the groaning floorboards. She rifled through books stacked on the oak table, pulling out a thin volume wrapped in thick leather. Turning the pages, her eyes darted left and right.

She stopped, and pulled her lips into a smile.

Holding open the book to me, she tapped her finger over an illustration.

"Is this the urn you saw?" she asked.

I took the book from her, and held it close to make out the picture. My heart quit for two beats.

An image of a malachite urn drawn in delicate strokes of ink filled the page. The same malachite urn that existed in both my dream, and in Fate's study.

"This is incredible," I said. "But what does it mean?"

She sat next to me, putting her cold feet against my legs. She shivered pulling the duvet over her naked body.

"While you've been off arguing with kings and getting eaten by vampires, I've been busy researching. I came across this last night." She ran her finger across the squished letters below the illustration, reading aloud, "the urn is the most powerful of its kind. It's a vessel for trapping the mightiest of spirits."

"Such as deities," I said.

"What if this is where Fate trapped Clotho and Lachesis?"

My heart pounded, and relief flooded my veins.

"It would make sense. Why keep your weakness far away where you can't monitor its safety? That's why Fate never worried about us freely traipsing about meadows and valleys this whole time. What did he have to worry from us, if the only thing that could end him was right beside him?"

Hope started to sprout in me. The slimmest of light shone through the black. A long shot, sure, but at least we stood a chance.

Laila's joy melted, and she rubbed the back of her neck.

"Rumpel, you said these dreams changed once you rescued me. After you deepened your deal with Fate."

"Yes, and?"

She bit her lip now.

"What if when Fate gave you his powers, he left something more behind? Like a tether. A piece of himself. And when you bargained the second time, the tether strengthened?"

"What are you saying?"

"I think you two are linked more than you realize. He must have imparted a piece of his being in your that night he cut his scissors into your hand."

A cold sweat broke out on my forehead, and down my back. I swallowed hard, but my throat was so dry I almost gagged.

"You think our souls are entwined?"

She nodded.

"It explains everything. It explains the shadow within you. Why the Oracle, or even Darius, couldn't see past this shade. It's a piece of Fate, safeguarding this secret from you. He wants you and Rose to replace his sisters. With blood and magic, he's created a family bond stronger than blood alone. All he needs is to tether Rose as he did you, then this new trinity of destiny will be complete."

You boy, are destined for a dual spirit, Mina's voice echoed, predicting my future. Predicting me binding myself to Fate through blood and magic as Laila said.

A violent chill rolled deep in my gut. Laila took my hand, and squeezed. Joy and hope blazed in her eyes, calming my unease.

"But, what does this have to do with me having dreams of the urn? Why do his sisters call to me?"

She thought.

"Family," she said. "Because of Fate, you all share the same blood. He tethered you to himself, and unknowingly to his sisters as well. That was his mistake, the bastard. And his greed in making that second bargain with you only strengthened this tether. Somehow when you sleep, you open yourself to their pleas."

I saw it now. The beautiful horror of it all. We were all connected through little links and chains. Like individual rivers all united by a vast ocean.

"Within you lies the key," I whispered the Oracle's words.

Clarity descended upon me, terrifying clarity.

"This was the key, Rumpel. This is what you hoped to discover. If we are right, if Clotho and Lachesis are trapped in that urn, that means we stand a chance to win."

I swept her into my arms and held her tight.

"Laila, you are the cleverest of any I know," I said, letting her go. "You've brought hope back to me."

She smiled.

"Knowing this now, how do we proceed?" she asked.

"Like everything is status quo. We continue to the portal, and after that...It will take wits, bravery, and probably a hearty dose of stupidity."

"We can count Fate's unawareness of this link as our luck."

My stomach twisted, and fear chased away my exuberance. Fear not for myself. I reached for Laila's hand, and rubbed my thumb over her knuckles.

"If we're wrong, if he catches us trying to thwart him, he will destroy you and Tristan. There won't be anything more I can do to protect you."

"We've both already agreed to fight beside you. We fully knew the risks when we started this journey. There's no turning back now."

My throat tightened. I traced the spot on her bare chest where Fate had removed that glowing thread from her.

"He won't give you back your soul." My words were soft, terrified.

She cupped my face and leaned her forehead against mine. I closed my eyes, breathing in her scent of citrus and orange blossom.

"I told you I would be with you until the end."

I kissed her, wanting to savor her taste, fearing I would never taste her again.

Linked beings share the same fate, you see.

I KNOCKED ON TRISTAN'S DOOR.

Time was our enemy now, and the dwindling hours until the blood moon churned my stomach.

I pounded again, the lock clattering with my every strike.

Why isn't he answering the bloody door?

"Tristan!" I yelled. "Get out of that bed and open up."

A hand squeezed my shoulder. I turned, facing Laila. Worry deepened the lines of her face.

"Rose isn't in her room," she said. "I don't know where she is."

My pulse quickened.

"Dammit! We haven't the time for this."

I beat against the door, the wood rough against my open palms.

"Tristan! I swear, you better open this minute."

Still no answer.

"Did something bad happen?" Laila asked. "What if Fate..." Her words dwindled, but I could guess her fear. What if Fate found out what we planned? What if he took them?

"Stand aside."

Waving my hands, I blasted the door open, the wood cracking against the stone wall. Ink dripped over the desk and puddled on the floor next to his toppled chair. Melted wax scented the air.

Anxiety twisted my stomach. I didn't like this.

I went to his bed and pulled back the duvet. Empty.

Laila checked in corners and behind velvet curtains. Also empty.

"Are we too late?" Laila asked, tearing through the wardrobe.

"I hope not," I whispered.

Sweat covered my brow as nerves threatened to take over. We had to find them.

Whistling came up the stairs, accompanied by heavy footsteps. A servant walked in carrying a pitcher of steaming water. I gripped him by his shoulders, causing him to drop the pitcher. It smashed at our feet, hot water flooding the floorboards.

"Where is he?" I screamed, digging my fingers into his arms.

His face twisted in fear. I squeezed him harder.

"Wh...who sir?"

"Dammit, the boy and the girl."

He seemed to shrink, and his lips quivered. Fool. Could he not answer me a simple question?

"Are you mute?"

"No, sir, I don't know where they are!"

"I don't believe you."

He whimpered like an eight year old child.

"Let him go," Laila said. "We must search elsewhere."

I couldn't risk anything. I had to press him for any information his penile brain might hold. I would not suffer fools.

"How much did they pay you for your silence? If you don't tell me, I will rip out your liver!"

"I didn't pay him anything," Tristan's voice cut behind me.

Relief flooded me like a balm.

I loosened my grip, and the man fell to the ground. He scrambled to regain his footing, then tore out of the room.

I spun on my heel and faced Tristan. I wanted to run up and hug him, to tell him the good news, but I stopped.

His gaze bled with chilled rage.

I decided to ignore it. There was no time for one of his tantrums now.

"Thank God. We thought we lost you," I said. "Now's not the time to be wandering about."

He didn't respond, just pressed his thumbs harder against his fists. He flattened his lips, irritation thinning them further.

"We need to go," Laila said, her words cautious. No doubt she also noticed Tristan's odd temper. "We think we know where Clotho and Lachesis are trapped. We have a fighting chance, Tristan. Isn't that wonderful?"

No emotion, beside contempt. I'd seen him upset before, but never this cold.

I knew our meeting with Mishkin yesterday had upset him, but I hoped his rage would have calmed by now.

Remaining silent he closed the door behind him, and locked it shut. Fury darkened his expression, deepened it, making the hairs on my neck raise.

I didn't like this. I hoped he hadn't done something stupid.

"Tristan, where's Rose," I asked, my voice calm. I didn't want to push him off the edge he seemed to stand on.

"She isn't here," he said with clipped words.

"Then where is she?" Laila asked.

He glared at her, boiling rage, raw and dangerous glinting behind his eyes.

"She is safe," he replied. "Safe from you. Safe from both of you," he snapped.

My confusion grew, and I cursed Mishkin, and myself, for causing this rift. Especially with how he now glared at his mother. I never wanted him to look at her that way.

"I know you are angry at your mother and I concerning Mishkin, but this is not the time. We can't lose faith in one another when we are so close to the end."

He shook his head and sneered.

"Is that what you think I'm upset about?"

"Is it not?"

He chuckled.

"I tried to understand all your little glances, and cryptic mutterings. I tried to reason your delight in your cruelty towards Mishkin. Yet, an itch remained in the back of my head, that there is something deeper to you both."

"Let's discuss this on the way," Laila cut in.

"NO!" he shouted. "We will discuss this now." He stepped towards us and slammed an old book on the table. "You see, I know."

I thought the book rubbish, but Laila's eyes widened and her mouth fell open. She gripped my hand, and cold sweat moistened her palms.

"And what exactly do you know?" I asked him, playing his game.

"Rumpel..." Laila breathed, terror pulling on her voice. "That's Edward's diary."

The ground shifted beneath my feet, and my throat turned to sand.

Bile rose as my stomach twisted, and I heard nothing but the rush of blood in my ears.

This is what Laila and I feared.

"Tristan," I choked. "Let us explain." I couldn't find my voice. It drowned in my panic. I couldn't lose him. Not like this.

I stepped towards him. I had to fight.

He drew his sword and pointed it at my chest. He might as well have driven it right into my heart.

Hatred glared in his gaze at me. In that heartbeat I was a stranger to him, no memory of me existing at all. A thing with no warrant for mercy or forgiveness. My core buckled with sickness, and mostly at myself. Laila and I were both fools to think we could keep this secret from him.

"You've said quite enough," he snapped. "All you've ever done is lie to me. I don't want to hear another twisted word fall from your lips. Father explained everything very clearly in his diary."

I couldn't help but let out a dark chuckle. Tristan pressed his point against my chest.

"Your father the truthful one. There's a laugh."

His eyes flared and he forced the blade deeper, but not enough to break my skin. Not yet, anyway. Cold sweat beaded on my temples. He couldn't kill me, but the idea stung no less.

"You killed him," he spat. "You killed him and took everything from him. You took me."

Red blotched his skin now, and his anger caused him to tremble.

"Tristan," Laila said. "It's not what you think. We are not who we were then. And even then, we were slaves to circumstances out of our control."

Her voice made me want to weep.

Though strong and clear, I could detect a quiver at the end of her words. We both fought for Tristan. For his understanding and forgiveness. But how could he understand what was so clearly monstrous? How could he forgive what was disgusting? We asked an impossible thing.

"It's not what I think?" he said to his mother. "Are you saying you didn't trade me for silks and rouge? That you didn't make a deal with this *thing* for him to spin straw into gold? You destroyed my father."

I couldn't bare the venom he spat at Laila. Especially when I was entirely responsible. I was the one that corrupted her, that made her make such awful choices. If any of us deserved to lose Tristan, it was me.

"If you want someone to blame, blame me alone," I said. "I admit it. I tempted her to bargain for you. I offered her choices that only served my own gain. I am the one that buried my blade deep into your father's chest. Your mother was my victim."

"Rumpel, don't," Laila whispered.

Loathing stiffened his features. The sharp point of his sword bit my skin, daring to pierce me. For two seconds I saw his father when he had run his sword into my chest.

"I don't care," he told me. "It doesn't wipe away her sins. My father was a great man, and you both deceived him, as you deceived me. You, Pater, are a creature as he said."

My own rage blazed and raced through my veins, hot and livid.

"You think me a creature?" I asked. No, roared! I gripped his blade, cracking the metal until it disintegrated to dust. Tristan's eyes widened, and he gulped. Lunging at him, I pushed him against the wall and pressed my arm into his chest. Clutching his wrist I struck it against the plaster so he couldn't pull out his dagger. "Your father was the creature. A cold, heartless prick."

He spit in my face. I thought my heart ripped out and stomped beneath his boot.

"I will never believe you," he said.

Laila gripped my shoulders and pulled me back. Her chest rose and fell in heavy breaths. Red flushed her cheeks, but from fear or grief I wasn't sure. Perhaps both. I hated the despair radiating from inside her soul the most. It longed for her son's forgiveness.

"Tristan, you are right," she said. "We have lied to you. I did give you up, I did take Rumpelstiltskin's deal. But it wasn't only for a crown. It was to save my own life from your father."

Tristan sneered and shook his head.

"More lies. He said he gave you a test, a chance to prove your abilities. He was helping you be praised for your talents."

I laughed fully now.

"Is that how he put it? How politely worded."

"What do you mean?"

"Because it sounds far better than the truth," I snapped. "He wasn't doing your mother any favors. His test was a cruel trick. A way to expose a fraud. He didn't expect her to succeed, he wanted to drown her in suffering before he chopped off her head. I suppose he left out all these pesky details in his grand opus."

Tristan bit his lip, as if thinking. He crossed his arms tight over his chest.

"I don't believe it."

"Your father was a sadistic monster," Laila continued. "He threw me in a dungeon filled with straw and a spinning wheel to mock me. He told me if I could spin all the straw into gold by morning, I would win my life. It was all a game to him. Until Rumpelstiltskin came to me and gave me a chance to fight for my freedom. When you drown in fear, you will do whatever it takes to survive."

He rubbed his face with his hand, not meeting our gazes.

"He abused your mother, Tristan. He locked her away, took her hope, and wanted to break her. I offered her a way out. We both didn't know the consequences."

"Because you were so merciful to ask for children as a simple payment," he spat.

I took a breath. I preferred to press the pain of my past deep into my depths. I loved the shroud of mystery, and the coldness I could use to numb my heart. Now, I had to peel away my layers, and finally reveal to him the truth of who I was. Who I used to be.

"I was the heir of Barschloss Manor. My family was close cousins to your father, serving the crown for centuries. Until Edward decided our blood was too close for his comfort. He rode to our home during the night, and as I hid, I watched him drive a blade into my father's chest. He struck the name Rumpelstiltskin from all histories, taking my lands and title. I was an outcast."

Tristan's arms loosened, and fell to his sides.

"Vengeance overcame any sanity that remained within me. That's how I met Fate. That's how I received my power. Fate promised I would achieve my revenge. He helped me see how to win. I had to destroy Edward's legacy. You."

"So your answer was to punish an innocent woman and child to help your own grief?"

"Yes," I replied. "I don't expect you to understand, but you asked for the truth. I'm sorry for every lie I ever told, for all the pain I've caused. I'm sorry to both you and your mother. I'm sorry instead of rebuilding my life fresh, I further cursed my family name."

I sat on the bed. I didn't remember sitting down.

Tristan's rage cooled. His eyes softened, and he looked at his feet.

"I was there," he breathed. "Fire destroyed most of it. Grim place."

"Where are you talking of?"

"Barschloss," he said. My heart stopped for two beats. "I discovered it when I ran away. I...I found a jaw of a child."

My eyes burned. The heat of the flames singed my skin, and the smoke filled my nose. The screams made me shiver.

"Madeline," I whispered. "My sister. Edward locked my mother and sister in an upstairs room. He lit the curtains ablaze. I tried to fight back through the flames, but I couldn't reach them. Their cries haunt me still."

His skin whitened. Laila's eyes misted red. I hoped I had reached him.

He pressed his hands against his head, and shook it back and forth. My heart sunk.

"Maybe it's true my father was cruel," he said. "But you were both vile. Have you ever even felt remorse?"

"You have no idea," I replied. "Guilt is what drives every beat of our hearts."

Laila marched to him, rolling up her sleeve.

"Maybe this will help you understand. You seem to think we cackled and rejoiced in our wrongs. We both fought to right our mistakes in the past, as we are fighting now."

She held out her arm to him. A thin scar trailed down her skin. I remembered the night Edward maimed her. I wanted to kill him.

"I'm sure your father mentioned making a new deal in his diary."

Tristan nodded, stiffly.

"I begged your father not to take it, but he wouldn't listen. He was too proud, too cruel. I grabbed the quill from him, trying to protect you. He ripped it from my grasp and tore the point down my arm, leaving me with this scar. This scar I wear proudly. It's proof I tried to save you."

She pulled down her chemise from her left shoulder, displaying her bare skin. A fine mesh of claw marks scarred her flesh. I'd never noticed them before.

"These are the nails of the Furies that dragged me away for breaking my deal with Rumpelstiltskin. He and I both tried to stop it from taking effect, but the magic was too strong. Too binding." She paused, and breathed deeply. "I let you go. He promised he would raise and protect you, and I went with the Furies to suffer my punishment. It's easy to promise something away that doesn't exist, but it's impossible to not fight for something you love. You see, Tristan. We have always fought for you."

Shock overcame Tristan's face and his eyes cleared.

Laila's bravery shook me to my center. The pain this woman endured, that I caused her to suffer, revolted me. I owed them both more than my soul to repay what I had done.

I cleared my throat.

"Tristan, we both have blood on our hands. We both have made mistakes, but we have tried to right them. My rage at your father, my vengeance, cost me love. Don't make the same mistake in letting your own anger rule you. All we want is your forgiveness, and one day, we hope to win back your trust."

He nodded his head, still not meeting my gaze.

"There's one thing I don't understand," he said. "You told me Fate killed my father, but now you admit it was you. What role did Fate truly play in all this?"

"Everything," I said. "Fate is the one that put the idea in your father's head that our family bond was too close. He gave me the power so I could enact my vengeance on Edward. He planned your birth, that you would be born with the blood necessary to break Rose's curse."

We all stood in silence.

"Are we ok?" Laila asked Tristan.

"No," he said. "But we will be."

"That's all I ask," I said. I wanted to embrace him, but decided against it.

"Now you know the complete truth, you know more what's at stake," Laila said. "You know the power we face, the manipulative force that wants us to crumble. Fate will enslave Rose to himself if we are not back in time. Now, where is she?"

Alarm overcame his features.

"I sent her to Lord Hochstein," he said.

Bile rose up my throat and my gut pitted. I hadn't heard that name in decades.

"Is that the older man you spoke too?" I asked.

"Yes, that's who gave me the diary. He's my godfather."

I knew I recognized the face. It was Edward's closest friend. Last I saw him he was a sniveling teenager.

"He's a scoundrel," I said. "Lord Hochstein supported Edward in killing my father. He is only after power, and is using you. He enjoyed the comfortable life he led with Edward. Nothing would please him more than to be your minister. He is angry I altered the line of succession against his favor."

Tristan took a step back.

"And I sent Rose right to him," he whispered, horrified.

"He knew giving you that journal would poison you against us, and turn you to him. We must get her out."

He went white and hung his head low. I felt for him. I knew how it felt to be played the fool. It sunk in your stomach and made you want to hide for an eternity.

"I thought I was doing the right thing, and in the end, I only put us all further in danger."

"It is human. We all have done what we thought was right to find later it a mistake. All we can do is move forward," Laila said.

I couldn't bear to tell him the gravity of his error. I only hoped we all survived it.

CHAPTER TEN

Lord Hochstein's castle stood rotting and broken at Schloss Hofbrunn.

We pressed through thick bushes and lifted our feet over grass that reached our calves. The putrid stink seared my nostrils from the defunct fountains, the basins filled with viscid slime and sour water.

Wild things lurked in the gardens that were now jungle.

We kept our steps soft circling the once magnificent structure. I searched for a suitable entrance, inspecting the windows first. Several of the glass circles of the leaded windows were already broken, paper stuffed inside to keep out the cold.

Possible entry point, but not ideal.

A door would be better, but the clinging ivy obscured much of the house.

"Will he harm her?" Tristan whispered.

"He wants to stay in your good graces. He won't be cruel to her, unless we raise his suspicions. Hopefully we will catch him unaware, making this quick and clean."

Tristan shuddered.

"I can't wait until we can get her out of there."

"I can't wait to snap his neck."

I made to continue on, when he gripped my wrist, stopping me.

"Don't kill him," he said. "Lord Hochstein might have manipulated me, but he is still my godfather. It's best to leave him to his mediocrity."

I frowned.

"But it would be much simpler..."

"Tristan is right," Laila cut in. "Death is not always necessary. Besides, from the looks of things, I doubt he has any servants except a valet and kitchen maid."

I didn't like this. Death was certain, mercy meant complications.

I made to argue, but Tristan put out his hand, hushing me.

"This is my mess, and this is how I want to repair it," Tristan added.

"Fine, but if he makes one wrong move, I'll break his spine."

We crept along the edge of the manor, every room dark except for two on the bottom floor. Feeling through the vines, I found a side door and turned the handle.

Locked.

I flicked my wrist, and the metal latch opened with a soft click. We slid through, finding ourselves in the kitchens. Stale bread and molding cheese sat on a chipped, china plate.

Weaving through we walked up a narrow flight of stairs that opened into a library. Mildew thickened the air from rotting books and tapestries. We navigated around the bleak furniture, opening another door that led out to a great hall.

Voices spilled out with soft light beneath a door several rooms away. Hochstein and Rose's voices.

Tristan started to bolt, but I grabbed his leather belt and pulled him back.

"What in blazes are you doing?" I whispered.

"I'm going to rush in there, grab her, and run out. Quick and clean, like you said."

I pulled my hand down my face.

"Don't let his graying hair fool you. Lord Hochstein is a trained soldier, and deadly. If you barge in there, he will take Rose hostage for sure. He knows she is your weakness, and he will use that to his advantage. Don't act rash."

He sighed.

"Then what do you suggest?"

I thought.

"You walk in," Laila said. "You walk in like everything is fine, and you thank him for his service. Don't give him any reason to suspect you. Rose might be your weakness, but you are his."

Her intelligence made my heart beat more for her than I knew capable.

"I don't know." He crossed his arms.

"He believes you are on his side," I said. "Play the part. Make him feel he's won."

"And then what?"

"Make a reason for you to leave," Laila said. "You will be able to walk out of there without a cross word spoken."

He tapped his fingers against his bicep and chewed the inside of his mouth.

"And if not? What if he insists we stay?"

"We will distract him so he leaves, then you can get Rose out. Break through the window if you have too. Since you insist on sparing him, this is the only way," I said.

He rubbed the sweat from his forehead on his sleeve.

"Can you do this?" Laila asked.

He sucked in a breath, and lifted his chest. He squared his shoulders and fixed his tousled hair, picking out an ivy leaf.

"Yes," he said. "For her."

The parquet creaked and groaned as we neared Rose and Hochstein. Their voices grew clear as they spoke of riding. I prayed their crackling fire would muffle our footsteps.

Laila and I pressed our backs against the wall, and I nodded to Tristan to open the door. He took another breath, gripped the handle, turned it, and walked in.

Their conversation ceased. My heart pounded into my throat.

"Tristan!" Rose exclaimed. Fabric rustled as she stood and, I assumed, embraced him. "Thank the gods you're safe. I've been caught between anger and fear for you. Sending me off in the dead of night with no explanation. I'm not a frail creature to be protected, I could have stayed and helped you."

"Sorry, I panicked," he replied. "Everything is alright, now."

"She is a fine woman, Tristan," Lord Hochstein's smooth voice came. My blood boiled. "She has true fire. We've enjoyed chatting while we waited word from you."

I scooted hard along the plaster, moving closer to the door.

"I'm happy to hear it," Tristan replied.

"He's told me everything about Rumpelstiltskin and Laila. I had no idea of their pasts," Rose said.

"I thought it best she know," Hochstein responded.

"Yes, he's been very thorough." I detected a hint of false appreciation in her voice.

"It's been a difficult day for all of us," Tristan said.

Someone patted a shoulder.

"I'm glad you've finally accepted the truth," Hochstein said. "I can't imagine your pain realizing what your mother, and that *thing*, did to your father."

I curled my fingers into fists and squeezed tight, pretending I squeezed his neck.

"Still," Rose said. "I would like to hear their version of the events. It takes two sides to make one coin."

I dared a step closer, straining to hear. Laila's silver ring I kept in my pocket slipped out of a hole. My heart leapt, and ice flooded my veins. Horror filled Laila's face.

Metal rang clear and piercing as it struck the parquet at my feet.

"Did you hear that?" Hochstein asked.

I knelt down and picked up the ring, putting it deep in my inner coat pocket. I wiped cold sweat from my face.

"Must be a cat," Tristan said.

A pause.

"Yes, of course. Irritating creatures." I wasn't sure Hochstein sounded completely convinced. "Tell me, have the villains been apprehended?"

"Of course," he replied. "Put up a fight, but I overcame them both. Left them bound and awaiting the proper punishment back at the inn. Speaking of which, we really must be getting back before they escape. Thank you for your hospitality."

"So soon? You didn't even tell me how you achieved such an impossible feat. Rumpelstiltskin's powers are legend."

Shit. Suspicion thickened in his voice. Tristan faltered.

"I'm sure you learn a thing or two about a man's weaknesses when you live with them your whole life," Rose replied, breaking the tension.

If I could have raced up and kissed her, I would have.

"True," Hochstein replied.

"Yes, Rumpelstiltskin is no match for me," Tristan responded. "I can't waste anymore time, I will send a letter to you with further instructions later. Thank you for your loyalty and service."

"Of course, anything I can do to support your father's memory," he said. "But, before you go, one drink could do you no harm?"

"Maybe next time."

"Indulge me," he said, his words firm. "Capturing a beast like Rumpelstiltskin is a moment worth celebrating! We will toast to your father."

Silence.

"Fine, but make it quick," Tristan said.

Wine poured into goblets.

"To Edward, the rightful king, and to his son, who overcame this century's greatest sorcerer."

Goblets struck a table as they put down their cups.

"Thank you, Lord Hochstein. Until we meet again."

Footsteps neared the doors, and my tight stomach loosened along with my shoulders.

"You disappoint me," Lord Hochstein said, his voice cutting. "I had thought better of you. I had thought you'd understand. But you dare disrespect your father's memory by toasting to him, when you still believe in that monster! After you know everything he did to him."

Metal cracked against a wall, and I had to assume he threw his goblet.

"What are you talking about?" Tristan asked.

Lord Hochstein laughed.

"I'm not a fool," he said. "You can't overcome a thing like Rumpelstiltskin as you claim. Impossible. You lie. I know you lie, because a beast like that has no weakness. Trust me, I've long searched."

"Don't listen to him, Tristan. Let's go," Rose said. "He has no weapons. He has no guards. We can leave."

"You are right. I have no guards, but that doesn't mean I don't have an ace to play."

My hairs stood on the back of my neck.

"Idle threats," Tristan said. Their shadows grew as they approached the door. I was ready to snap us all to safety once I could touch them.

"I tried to show you the truth," he called after them. "Even your father's own words you spit on. I will not let you throw away your crown, or piss on your father's memory because of your naive mind."

Tristan and Rose's steps stopped.

"I've come to realize the truth is complicated," Tristan said. "In fact, truth doesn't exist. Only opinion and intent. I've decided to believe those intent to change for the better."

"Wicked boy," he hissed. "They've twisted you all up. I will set you back on course. I swore an oath to your father to look after you, and I intend to keep it. Come out, come out, creature...I know you're there."

I cursed beneath my breath. The game was over.

Resigning myself, Laila and I walked in together. Gratefulness filled me for the chance to speed this process up, and end his nonsense. We needed to get going to the portal before the blood moon rose.

Glee lit Hochstein's face. Terror froze Tristan's. And Rose, I didn't like the dark circles beneath her eyes. In fact, she seemed awfully pale.

"How good of you to finally join us. I hate eavesdroppers."

"As much as you hate housekeeping, it appears," I quipped. "Money problems?"

He ground his teeth.

"The results of your betrayal of the crown. I lost everything that day."

I laughed.

"You have no right to talk about betrayal to me," I ground out.

"We were right to kill your father. Waste of a man. A disease. His own son sold his soul to the devil."

I fought everything in me that wanted to leap at him and tear out his heart. But I didn't, for Tristan.

"You walk on thin ice," I warned.

His eyes flashed with malice. He turned to Laila. She stood taller, not betraying any fear of him.

"And you, Edward's own wife, turned demon's whore."

Laila lunged at him and struck him across the face. Blood trickled out of his nose, dripping over his lips and chin.

"I rather be a whore than a sadist's wife," she spat.

I gripped her arm and pulled her back, fearing she would claw his eyes out. It pained me to do so, as no spectacle would have pleased me more.

"Come on, let's go," I said. "He's not worth our energy."

I couldn't believe I said such a thing. What was Tristan making me become? Tenderhearted?

"You don't want to do that," he said.

I chuckled. Fool.

"You know better than anyone there's no stopping me. You've just admitted I have no weakness."

He raised an eyebrow, and nodded.

"True, but I think you much rather make a deal with me."

Rose lost her footing, but Tristan held her up. She motioned she was fine, but the sweat on her forehead said otherwise. We needed to get out before we missed the moon.

"No thanks, you have nothing I want."

We neared the door.

"Make a deal with me, or Rose dies."

We stopped, and I faced him. I made sure the others were well behind me.

"What are you going to do? If you want her, you're going to have to come through me. My magic if far quicker than your blade."

Rose pressed her fingers between her eyes. Something wasn't right.

"True, your magic is strong, but it's useless against the poison of the Veluria plant."

My stomach twisted and my pace quickened. Tristan helped Rose to a chair.

"What's happening to me?" Rose asked, her voice dry.

"Sorry, dear, but this was the only way to get Rumpelstiltskin to listen."

"One must ingest poison, or have it scratched into their skin," I said.

He rolled his eyes.

"Why do you think I had us make a toast? Once I was certain Tristan lied, I played my ace. She has twenty minutes, at best."

I swallowed hard.

"You bastard!" Tristan roared. "I trusted you!" He lunged at him and held his dagger against his throat. "Fix this, or I swear I'll...I'll kill you. I've done it before."

I'd never been prouder of Tristan, but the time for such tactics was long gone.

Hochstein only chuckled.

"Innocent boy. Naive boy. Kill me and Rose dies, too," he spat.

"Tristan, we should listen. Come away," Laila said.

He continued glaring, pressing the blade against his throat, then backed away. Hochstein rubbed his neck.

"Let's get this over with. What game are you wanting me to play?" I asked.

"As I said, make a deal with me, and I will give her the antidote. Only I know where it is."

"Fine."

He smiled, a disgusting, twisted smile.

"First, remove the woman and the boy. I don't want to risk any more interference from Tristan, or worse, have him inadvertently injured. As for Laila, I want her alive for what I have planned once this is over."

I didn't know what he planned, and the danger in his voice sent a chill to my toes. But, I agreed it was best they both be safe and out of the way. I gripped their wrists before they could protest, and sent them to the kitchens. Snapping my fingers I locked the kitchen doors.

With them gone, I rushed to Rose. I knelt by her side and took her hand.

"Stay with me," I said. "It will be ok."

Her hand felt like a cadaver, cold and waxy.

"I'm fine," she said.

She was definitely not.

Hochstein's shadow fell over us.

"It's attacking her system now. First will be a cold sweat followed by chattering. Death only comes at the end, once they start to pray for angels to end their pain. Beautiful poison. It makes a believer out of the staunchest atheist."

I ground my teeth and stood, facing him. How dare he play with the life of an innocent girl. But then, I too, had done the same to Laila.

"What do you want?" I growled. "To be king? To have your wealth restored?"

He shook his head.

"Being king is too much work. All those documents to read and sign. What a bore! As for my wealth, that will be restored to me once

Tristan is back on the throne. My lands, my titles, my life of ease. Tristan is my saving grace, and why I won't harm a hair upon his head."

"Why through him, when you can have it now through me?"

He almost seemed offended.

"Unlike you, *monster*, I do have a heart. I am his godfather, and I promised Edward to serve his line until my dying breath. I will see Tristan reinstated, and enjoy the reward of my loyalty."

I shook my head. This man was insane. But I suppose to be Edward's friend, you'd have to be.

"Tristan will never go along with your plans. Especially now."

He shrugged.

"True, but that's only if he remembers. As you know, there is a potion for everything. A few drops and he will forget anything other than how his loving godfather saved him from the evil sorcerer Rumpelstiltskin," he said. "You took everything from me. You forced me to live in squalor thanks to your treason. Now, I will do what Edward couldn't. I will end you."

I clenched my jaw tight until pain swelled in my ears.

"You seem to think yourself very capable in defeating me."

Rose moaned. Blue tinged her lips and the tips of her fingers.

"Let the girl go. Your quarrel is with me," I said.

He shook his head.

"Not until our deal is finished."

He poured wine into a silver cup, then reached into his inner pocket and pulled out a small vial. Popping the stopper off, he emptied the thick, black concoction into the wine, swirled it a second or two, and handed it to me.

Magic pulsed through the metal. Dark magic.

"I want you to drink this."

"More poison? This is a waste of my time. I can't be poisoned."

I sat the goblet on the table.

"I know," he said. "This is something more intricate than poison. Took ages to find. You see, the moment Tristan said he defeated you, I knew he lied. Contracts and swords do nothing against an immortal. Edward should have been smarter when he crossed you."

"And you are? Can we hurry this along?"

He narrowed his eyes.

"This will arrest your magic, rendering you mortal. If a beast has no weakness, then you must give him one. For once the playing field is made equal."

My smug expression drooped, and my arms fell to my side. Victory shined in his gaze.

"No," I said. "I won't accept this bargain. I won't drink that."

He looked to Rose. She shook, and clawed at the pillows as pain stiffened her body.

"She's slipping away," he said. "The convulsions will be next. Absolute agony."

My heart raced. I drowned in despair of not knowing what to do. I couldn't risk dying, leaving Laila's soul still in Fate's possession. I couldn't risk Rose dying, failing Fate completely.

"There must be something else you want? I can give you anything." I hated how I begged. I never begged.

"You've already given me what I want," he said. "You brought Tristan out of hiding. You gave me a way back into the kingdom."

He scooted the goblet across the table towards me.

"Your immortality, or her life."

Blood rushed in my ears. My veins swelled with terror. Panic. I was frozen, standing in the shoes of countless others I had forced into equally impossible decisions. This was irony, I supposed.

"The monster is afraid," he said. "How droll."

A new emotion washed over me. Conviction. Decision.

Without thought, I lifted the goblet to my lips and downed it. I forced myself to swallow the liquid down, the cedar and plum of the wine faint against the bitterness of the potion.

I hated the smile pulling on his lips, but I refused for him to see me shudder.

I squared my shoulders, ignoring the metallic flavor still burning my tongue. Disregarding the fire searing my throat.

"I've appeased your request," I rasped. "Now let her go."

"Of course. Here's the antidote, as promised." He pulled out another small vial from his pocket. "All she has to do is drink it.

Edward and I used to have such fun together with these sorts of games. Life can be won, it's how hungry one is to fight."

He tossed the vial to Rose. She ground her teeth as she lifted her trembling arms into the air to catch it. She fumbled as the bottle struck her fingers, jumped to her lap, and slid off her satin gown and onto the Turkey rug. Bending forward to reach for the vial she clutched her stomach instead. She cried out and fell back on the couch, her breaths labored.

"Oh dear," he said.

Bastard.

I started for the vial to lift it to her lips when the room tilted. Or did I tilt? Heaviness weighed down my legs, like I trudged through deep mud. My shoulders slumped forward, and my spine refused to remain erect. I strained forcing my eyes to remain focused.

Frailty plagued my entire body.

I stumbled and Hochstein caught me. Digging into my upper arms, he held me up and leaned me against a table to steady myself.

"I imagine the sensations you are experiencing to be quite alarming. It's been awhile since you were a mortal man."

My mind swam making, it difficult to concentrate on his words. A dull haze clouded my usually clear and quick thoughts.

"A little lace wing and I've broken you as one does a wild stallion."

I blinked several times trying to rid them of dryness. My skin crawled, and I didn't like the sensation of vulnerability. I'd forgotten the weakness of mortality, the fragility of it all.

Anxiety clutched my fatiguing heart. I had to get the antidote to Rose. I tried to stand on my own, but my legs continued to tremble holding my own weight.

I tried to curse him, but even my voice seemed lost.

"It's not permanent, only temporarily arrested. But it will last long enough for me to make you bleed."

He drew his sword and sweat ran down my back.

He approached me and I staggered away towards the vial laying out of Rose's grasp. She writhed on the sofa now, her veins black against her gray skin.

I stumbled to the floor, crawling to the vial that would save her. I reached out, my fingertips almost grazing the bottle...

I screamed as he drove the point of his blade into my hand. Blood gushed out over my knuckles.

I looked up over my shoulder. Amusement glistened across his face.

"Are you just going to torment me?" I asked.

"I expected more from you," he said. "You are worthless without your powers, aren't you? A shivering rat waiting to be put out of its misery. It's time to accept your fate."

Accept my fate?

Rage pulsed through me hot and boiling. It churned and frothed as it coursed through my heart and into my soul. There, in a dormant part of my being, awoke forces I didn't know I possessed. Spirit and courage.

I refused to let him beat me.

Gathering my will, I centered on what strength remained in me, and forced myself to stand. I rose off the ground, lengthening my back, and squaring my shoulders.

"I will never accept my fate."

He laughed, and it only sought to strengthen my resolve. I had to fight. I had to fight for Rose. For Laila and Tristan. I had to fight for myself.

"This is too much," he said. "You are unarmed, you won't last a breath."

"A breath is all I need."

I backed up against an oak dresser, and grabbed at anything behind me I might use to defend myself. I cursed finding only a silver candelabra, but it would have to do.

"I love that glint of fear in your eyes. Edward described seeing the same in your father's before he ran him through."

He brought down his sword, and I held out the candelabra. Steel scraped silver as his blade struck the metal arms, preventing his blow from slicing into my shoulder.

Surprise overcame him. Then anger.

"A bit of silver won't help you for long," he said.

Holding the base tight with both hands I prepared for his next attack. My heart thrashed in my chest, and my arms shook. I hated my mortal body.

He lunged, and I caught his sword again, blocking him. He cut, and I grunted pushing him back, begging my body to do what I needed.

If I could get him away for only a second, I could get the vial to Rose. I dared a glance at her. She still stretched for the bottle on the carpet.

He ran at me, and I backed up. I toppled a chair in his path, but he kicked it out of the way. I swayed, my footing still not stable, and rummaged through the drawers of a desk. Anything better than a candelabra.

My blood pounded faster in my ears.

I gripped tight around the ivory handle of a letter opener. Hochstein came at me again. He sliced his sword through the air, and again I caught his blade in the tangle of silver arms. I twisted with all my might, trying to disarm him, while I thrust my letter opener towards his heart.

He cried out. Blood soaked his shirt, and I hoped...

"You satan's spawn!" he screamed.

Dammit. I only succeeded in nicking his skin.

He pulled his sword free, a new wave of anger seeming to roll through him as he sliced and cut at me.

My mind muddled with getting to Rose, sinking my blade into his heart, and saving my own life. How angered Fate would be if I were to die now and be cheated of my soul. My death would almost be worth that alone.

I took a vase and threw it at his head. It smashed at his feet, his thick boots pounding the shards into powder as he came after me.

He lunged again, and again, and I blocked with my candelabra and thrust with my makeshift dagger. My back pressed against a wall, and fear shot through me. There was nowhere else to retreat.

He snarled, his lips rising above his yellowing teeth. He brought his sword down hard, and the silver threatened to slip out of my sweating palm.

I caught Rose's glance. The life in her eyes dimmed. Still, she reached for the vial, her body convulsing now. She rolled off the chaise onto the floor, screaming and gripping her stomach. Her fingers quivered as stretched out her arm, barely touching the vial. She hadn't the strength to get close enough.

If she didn't get the antidote, she wouldn't last more than a few more minutes. I couldn't let it end this way.

Hochstein pressed harder into me. I ground my teeth together, forcing my strength into my muscles. Into the letter opener I thrust into his side. It slid beautifully in, and I loved the hot gush of his blood over my fingers.

He cried out, his sword slipping from his grasp. He gripped his side, cringing. Using the wall to brace me, I kicked my right foot into his stomach forcing him back.

My lungs burned and heart thundered as I ran to Rose. I bounded for the vial, hope bubbling in me. She just needed to hold on a minute more...

Something caught my foot. I was falling. Falling and striking the floor, my palms skidding across the Turkey rug.

Pain shot through my body as Hochstein kicked me in the gut, my throat seizing shut as I gagged from the shock. I clawed at the carpet, not letting the vial out of my sight. Another strike of agony as he kicked again. My stomach clamped, and I nearly retched as I tried to suck in a breath.

The vial became two vials as my vision blurred.

An awful crack sounded out as he crushed his leather heel into my nose. Hot metallic filled my mouth.

I rolled on my back, staring at Hochstein's livid face. Blood stained his shirt at the two points I struck him, but it obviously wasn't enough.

Holding his sword over me, he pressed it into my shoulder. I winced as the point bit my skin. His eyes lit with glee. He enjoyed this.

"Your blood is a rare sight, but I desire more."

He shoved his blade through my shoulder, piercing the carpet on the other side. I screamed from the searing pain, then choked on my own blood still rushing down my throat. He pulled out his sword, letting my blood run off the tip and drip to the floor.

I tried to scramble away, but he struck my thigh, shoving the blade deep into my muscle. The sharp sting rippled through me and I roared. My vision blackened for two heartbeats.

"Please," I rasped. I couldn't lose. I was so close to the vial.

I gripped my fingers into the fibers of the carpet, pulling myself towards Rose. Darkness clouded my vision, but I could still make out her form.

He stepped in front of me, blocking her from my sight.

"End it," I gasped.

I couldn't make out his expression.

"I want to watch you bleed," he said. "I want to watch your life drip out of your body."

He punctured the side of my abdomen, and I screamed as agony tore through me. Hot liquid pooled beneath my back. The world grew hazier. Darker.

I hoped Rose could forgive me. I prayed Laila and Tristan could absolve my sins. I tried to do it all for them, and all I did was fail them.

I coughed up bile and blood, my throat raw from the grit.

He placed the tip of his sword over my heart. He sunk it slowly into my skin, drawing out my suffering as long as he could. All my pain swirled together now.

"Burn in hell," he said.

I braced myself for death. In truth, I wished it to come. Anything to end this.

His blade fell from his hand. He stood rigid, and blood foamed at his mouth dripping onto my forehead. He wavered, then fell, his head striking the mantel with a crack.

Above me stood Rose, the empty vial in her left hand, and the ivory handled letter opener in her right. Lord Hochstein's blood drenched the blade and her fingers.

Black consumed me.

CHAPTER ELEVEN

Swift:

Noun: A light, adjustable reel for holding a skein of silk or wool

Adjective: Happening quickly or promptly

TRISTAN

"The bastard magicked the door locked!" Mother yelled. She forced her dirk between the door and jamb, wiggling the blade to pry open the lock. "I have to get to him. He's unarmed, and without magic..."

She shimmied faster, her knuckles turning white as she pushed all her strength into the dirk. The door remained sealed.

"I can't let him die."

My thoughts were only of Rose.

She started stabbing at the door, chips of wood flying into her hair.

My heart thrashing, I searched for something stronger. Sharper.

I rummaged through back rooms connected to the kitchens, my heart stopping finding an ax. Picking it up, I ran back to Mother.

"If the lock won't break, we will break the door," I said.

Gripping the handle, I swung it back over my shoulder, and forced it forward with all my strength. I struck the door, the blade lodging itself into the heavy pine. Placing my foot against the wall, I pulled the blade free and struck again.

And again.

And again.

Chopping, splintering, cracking...

The door shook with my every strike as I broke through the panels, as I ripped at the shredding wood.

Nothing would prevent me from rescuing Rose.

My back and brow sweaty, I threw down the ax and kicked my boot into the breaking door. Shards of wood exploded out, and Mother rammed her shoulder against what remained.

Freedom.

We both scrambled out onto the other side, racing over the stone floor and up the tight, winding staircase back to the great hall.

Relief calmed my heavy breaths as Rose ran towards us, alive. Until I noticed blood covering her hands and soaking into her gown.

I caught her, squeezing her arms, checking for the wounds causing her to bleed.

"Where are you hurt?" I asked.

Tears streamed down her cheeks and she trembled.

"This isn't my blood. It's Rumpelstiltskin you must help," she cried. "He's dying. You must come, now!"

Mother gasped, and my stomach tightened. Though there were times I wished for Pater's death, I'd never actually wanted it. Shame overcame me for ever being so petty, and immature.

We followed her, running together back to the sitting room.

I thought I would vomit. Firelight reflected off blood pooling and sinking into the parquet. Crumpled beneath the mantel lay Lord Hochstein's limp body, gore seeping from his cracked skull. His eyes remained open, but hollow.

Shattered glass crushed beneath my boots, and we navigated around the toppled furniture trying to reach Pater.

My throat seized shut as shock split through me. I wanted to turn away.

Pater lay lifeless on the Turkey rug. Crimson surrounded him like an aura, his own blood drenching the fibers beneath him.

Mother knelt beside him, her hands shaking as she ripped open his shirt, feeling around the wound on his shoulder and side.

My eyes burned.

She lowered her ear to his chest. Taking out her dirk, she pressed it below his nose. Steam fogged the blade.

She choked out a cry of relief.

"He's still breathing," she said.

"Of course I am," he rasped, his voice almost a whisper. "I'm not that breakable."

"You should be dead," she said. "I thought you were dead."

He winced as she placed his head in her lap and stroked his hair.

"I nearly was. A second more, and Hochstein would have driven his sword through my chest." He lifted his gaze to Rose. "You saved me."

I turned to her. She looked down at her feet, and shifted.

"Rumpelstiltskin risked his own life to get me the vial," she whispered, still trembling. "His resolve fueled my own. I pushed myself until I finally grasped the antidote. A blade lay beside it on the floor." She lowered her gaze. "I sank it into Hochstein's back." She closed her eyes, clapping her hand over her mouth. "But the sound. The resistance of his flesh against my blade..." She shuddered. "Being trained to kill is different from actually killing."

I embraced her. I remembered the first man I had stabbed. The sensation. The guilt. The thrill.

"It was self defense. If you didn't, you both surely would have died."

She pulled away and nodded.

Pater cringed and grunted trying to get up, but fell back against Mother.

"Rest," she scolded him. She wiped the blood off his face with her skirts.

"We haven't the time," he pushed out. "That vile potion is weakening, and I sense my magic already returning. I should appear less horrific soon enough. We need to release Clotho and Lachesis before it's too late. We only have an hour before the blood moon."

"Who are Clotho and Lachesis?" Rose asked. "Are they going to help us end the sorceresses?"

My throat went dry. Pater and Mother looked at each other.

"Why are you all silent?" she asked.

"It's time she learns the truth," Laila said.

"What truth? Tristan?"

Her expression made me want to shrivel beneath a rock.

I took her hands in mine, but I could not meet her gaze.

"Clotho and Lachesis are the names of the sorceresses who cursed you," I said.

Rose tore her hands out of mine and stepped back. Humiliation sunk my shoulders, and my heart. My cheeks flushed with the heat of embarrassment. I kept Rose in the dark about our entire mission, just as Mother and Pater had kept me from the truth of their past.

"You told me we were going to vanquish them for imprisoning me. For cursing my entire kingdom. Not that we were going to *rescue* them," she spat.

"I'm sorry," I whispered. "Releasing them is our only chance at survival, and humanity's freedom. They are the only way to stop our one true enemy. Fate, *Atropos*, their third sister."

Her chest rose and fell in heavy breaths, and she clenched her hands into fists at her sides.

I killed her trust in us. We all had.

"You lied to me. You all lied."

She stepped back again. And then took one more.

"There was no other way to get you to come," I said.

Horror twisted in her expression.

"And why did you need me to come? Am I the sacrifice you need?"

In a way she was.

"No," I said. "Not exactly."

Pain bled from her eyes, and she shook her head.

"This is insane. I'm leaving."

She made for the door, but I grabbed her wrist, stopping her.

"Get off me!" She tried to pry my hand off her arm.

"Fate wants to destroy free will," I said, holding her tighter and trying to avoid her nails and heels as she started to kick. "To take choice from all people and bury them beneath his rule. He detests humanity's freedom, believing it a gift we don't deserve."

"This is why you were imprisoned and cursed," Mother broke in. Rose stopped her attack on my knees, but her muscles remained tense beneath my grip. "In order to vanquish free will, he had to lock away his other two sisters. There must always be three to create the destiny of men. Fate needed two new sisters to create his new trinity. A spinner and a measurer, you and Rumpelstiltskin."

Her gaze fell to Pater.

"You and I are a perfect match," he told her. "That's why Clotho and Lachesis cursed you in an attempt to thwart fate from enacting his plan. Buried beneath miles of thorns and brambles, lost in sleep, you were worthless to him. That's why Fate manipulated Tristan's birth. He needed him to break the spell. His blood was the only way to wake you."

Her shoulders relaxed, and I let her slip from my grasp.

"I remember what they told me," she whispered. "'Forgive us. Sacrifices must be made for the greater good.'"

"Yes, the greater good of preserving free will for the world," I said. "Fate imprisoned them for their interference. That's why we must release them. Only they know how to stop him."

She bit her lip, as if considering my words. Anger washed it away, stiffening her brow.

"I still don't understand why I'm needed. Like some kind of offering served on a silver platter like a fatted calf."

Pater grunted as he stood, mother slipping beneath his arm to help him. He limped a step or two towards Rose.

She didn't back away.

"Offering is the wrong word," he said. "More like, a red herring."

Her eyes narrowed.

"Explain."

He held out his palm to her, his scar red and sinewy. Her eyes widened, but she didn't recoil.

"I made a deal with Fate. This scar is the result," he said. "I promised to bring you to him by the Blood Moon of Phlegethon. Tonight." He paused, as if trying to push away the pain from his wounds. "I never intended to keep that deal, but if Fate ever discovered we planned to thwart him..." His voice wavered. "We needed you to keep up the ruse. I never expected we'd cut it so close. Endangering you was never the intention."

Her face reddened, and eyes hallowed. Her fingers tightened into fists at her sides.

"I understand, but these women destroyed me. It cuts me to my core to help them, when they caused me such misery."

He took in a breath, as if trying to summon strength to fill him. To heal him.

"I know you consider them your enemy, but they never were. Fate was," he said. "Trust me, I experienced misguided rage myself. I always believed Tristan's father to be the cause of all my suffering, when in truth, it was Fate all along. He played me, as he played you. Clotho and Lachesis only did what was necessary to keep the world safe."

"Still—"

"This is the only way to be free," he cut her off, his voice stronger. "Fate chose you long ago, whether you like it or not. Just as he chose me. Now we both are left to pick up the pieces. If we stay together, we will succeed."

She crossed her arms and chewed the inside of her mouth.

"What if I don't agree? What if Fate discovers your betrayal? What then?"

I stepped forward, daring to meet her gaze. My heart squeezed with remorse, but I had to try and reach her.

"I will die," I said. "He will disembowel me as a punishment."

"I will lose my soul," Mother said, rubbing over her chest where Fate pulled out her life's thread. "Fate possesses it, and will sever it with his scissors damning me eternally."

She looked at Pater now. "And you?"

"I will be his slave, his pet, until he finds another suitable match in another millennia. I will have no hope, nor will the world."

"I know it's hard to accept," Mother said.

She nodded, her lips pressed thin.

"And the bargain you made? If you fail in your mission of ending his plot, and if Fate miraculously doesn't discover your treason, what happens?

"Laila and Tristan's lives will be spared," Pater said. "But you and I will weave the destiny of men for eternity. We will be his family, and humanity will lose free will."

She clenched her jaw. I could only imagine the questions and fears swirling in her mind. I could barely believe it myself when Mother and Pater first told me. The entire concept bordered insanity and horror.

"I should have told you," I said. "We all should. I believed myself protecting you by hiding the truth. I was wrong. Please forgive me."

"I'm a grown woman. I'm not a child. I can make my own decisions. You should have given me the courtesy. Now I don't know what to believe, or whom."

That last sentiment cut me deep. I wanted her trust more than anything.

"I swear you know everything now."

She sneered and turned away. She paced between us and the door.

My life, and Mother and Pater's, rested in her decision. Besides her own life she was risking if she defied Fate. Though Fate couldn't force her, he always seemed to find a way to get what he wanted. It would only be a matter of time before she eventually fell.

"You told me you would do anything to end those that harmed you," Pater said. "Fate deserves the entirety of your wrath. The goal remains the same, it's just a different point of view."

She turned on her heels and faced us, taking in a deep breath. She loosened her crossed arms, letting them fall to her sides.

"In the end a threat is a threat," she said. "If I leave, it's clear my family and I remain in danger. Not to mention those I've come to call friends." She caught my gaze. "And those I've come to love."

I dared a step towards her. My pulse quickened, wanting to leap out of my throat.

"Will you still help us, then?" I asked.

She remained silent, as if thinking. I knew only seconds passed, but I believed it days.

"Let's take the bastard down," she said.

RUMPELSTILTSKIN

Ocean waves roared crashing against the white cliffs. Mist clung to my skin, and I tasted salt on my lips.

Sinking slowly beneath the horizon, the sun flushed in dark reds and deep pinks. Minutes remained until darkness would consume the sky, and the blood moon would rise.

Stepping on the razor edge of the cliff my pulse pounded. I lowered my gaze to the ocean below.

Sharp stone and jagged rock raced down, down, down disappearing into the frothing surf. Sweat beaded on my palms, and a thrill raced from my center up to my heart.

Beautiful. Deadly.

"Where is the portal?" Tristan yelled above the din. Wind tore through his hair, thrashing his locks against his eyes and forehead.

"You're looking at it."

He dared a step towards me, though he remained six feet behind. Rose stood by my side, her foot causing a pebble to break free and fall into the churning water.

"You can't be serious," Tristan said.

"When I told you we were going to the Cliffs of Sorrow, did you imagine a gentle hike?"

He bit his lip, and crossed his arms.

"How will we climb down?" Rose asked.

I laughed.

"Climb down? There's no time, princess. Besides, portals work best with a bit of velocity."

She raised her right eyebrow.

"Have you ever dropped something never to find it again?" I asked. "That's because it's fallen between a slice in time and space. This is the same concept, just on a larger scale."

"This is suicide," Laila said.

"Magic always takes a bit of madness to work."

"And how much madness will we require for this journey?"

She rested her hands on her hips and tapped her foot. I turned back to the rolling waves exploding in white foam. I couldn't stop a quiver tumbling in my stomach.

"You must stand on the cliff's edge, your back to the ocean. Outstretch your arms and fall back," I said.

"I don't know if I can," Tristan said.

He wiped sweat from his forehead, and his skin turned pale. I couldn't blame him, my own nerves on the edge of fraying.

Rose took his hand and held it tight.

"You must be brave," she said. "You must have faith."

"I always wanted to see the ocean," he said, stepping nearer the edge. "When the walls of my rooms tightened against me, I escaped to the ocean in my imagination. There I found absolute freedom. Now, it terrifies me, and I feel a fool."

"I'm afraid, too," Rose said.

"As am I," Laila added.

The sun fell deeper behind the horizon now, the dark reds fading into purples and blues. We didn't have much longer.

"You have no idea the dread filling me," I whispered. "But we must press on. Bravery isn't the lack of fear, it's overcoming it."

He sucked in a breath and nodded.

"I will go first," he said.

He pulled out of Rose's grasp.

"Keep focused on me. Don't look down," I said, directing him to the very edge of the cliff. The surf thundered below. "All you must do is think of where you want to go."

"And where's that?"

"Dream." I said. "Think of your dreams. We won't be far behind."

He nodded, then turned his gaze to Rose.

"If I do happen to break my neck, I want you to know I love you."

She smiled.

"I love you, too."

His hair flying and twirling around his head, he stretched out his arms. Closing his eyes, he breathed in, and fell back.

Down he went, vanishing into the sea. I could feel the magic of this place, and knew him safe, but it didn't stop my heart from twisting with anxiety and "what if's."

Rose turned against the ocean.

"Remember, think of Dream. Tristan will be there waiting for you."

She nodded and closed her eyes. Only a quarter of the sun remained above the surface, color washing the water. She leaned backwards, but I gripped her wrist and pulled her back from the ledge.

"What's wrong?" she asked.

"I don't know what to expect once we get on the other side. If there will be an opportunity. I wanted to thank you for saving my life," I said.

She nodded.

"That's what friends do," she said.

Warmth coated me. I hadn't had friends before. I wasn't used to this sensation.

She closed her eyes, stretched out her arms, and fell away, disappearing into the surf as Tristan.

Laila and I stood alone, wind rushing over our skin and fluttering our clothes. I put out my hand and she took it. I guided her to the edge.

"I hope we are right and this will be the end of the battle," she said.

I swallowed down the tightness squeezing my throat.

"Me too."

Pressing against her, I rested my palm on her chest. I skated over her skin, until I stilled over the spot where Fate pulled out her life's thread. Her soul.

"I will make this right," I said. "I can't bare the thought of him possessing your soul any longer."

She placed her hand over mine, moving me over her heart. It pulsed against my fingers.

"Fate might possess my soul, but you possess my heart."

"As you do mine."

It was an odd thought knowing both our souls were not ours. Her's remained with Fate as collateral for my return. And my own I promised to him in exchange for Laila's life. A cold sweat broke out across my back.

I wouldn't tell her what I suspected. What I feared about Fate and our linked elements.

"In case we fail, I want to tell you goodbye," I whispered.

She put her finger against my lips.

"We won't have a goodbye. I won't allow it."

She cupped my face, tracing my cheeks with her thumbs. I wove my fingers into her hair, her locks rippling wild and untamed in the wind. Her strength overcame me. Her resilience. Her beauty.

I kissed her deeply, rolling my tongue over hers. Our mouths moved in a hungry rhythm saturated with unfulfillable longing. And behind the need and the love, resided fear. A haunting specter forewarning we might never taste the other again.

We pulled apart, my lips hot and hers swollen.

"See you on the other side," she said.

Slipping out of my fingers, she fell back into the ocean.

The last sliver of sun hovered above the surface before me, stars shimmering with the approaching night behind.

Turning my back against the final rays of light, I stepped backwards until my heels met the edge of the cliff. A rock chipped off the edge, plummeting into the froth and foam.

I tried to still my thrashing heart. There was no returning after this leap.

Pushing thought away, I spread out my arms and leaned back into the wind. Gusts and gales tore through my hair and beat against my arms and legs. The cliffs rose higher towards the darkening sky, the thunder of the waves pounded my ears.

For two seconds I feared I made a mistake, and I braced for the shattering of my bones against the rocks.

Take me to Dream.

Water engulfed me, icy daggers piercing my skin. My chest constricted and my lungs burned, but from the magic in the portal, or from the ocean flooding my nostrils, I wasn't sure.

Deeper I fell, sunk, plummeted, through dark blues deepening to black. Numbness crept up my fingers and toes.

Panic set in, and I believed my lungs would soon burst from lack of breath.

Dream. Take me to Dream.

I stopped sinking. I floated. No, I rose. Rising up towards a light shining through the water.

Take me to Dream.

Surf and froth spat me out, throwing me hard against something unyielding. My teeth struck together and my skin scraped the rough surface.

Salt burned my eyes as I blinked, and I pressed into cold stone. I blinked again. Cobblestone. The ocean roar faded in my ears, replaced by the chirps of crickets.

I made it.

Standing, I righted myself. My clothes weighed down my shoulders, the fibers engorged with water. A sickening chill rolled down my spine standing on the same street from my first visit to Dream.

Laila, Tristan, and Rose wrung puddles out of their clothes.

Laila ran to me and embraced me.

"You're safe," she whispered in my ear.

"Of course."

I didn't want to let her go. The same fear from our kiss tore through me again that this would be the last time I ever held her.

"What do we do, now?" Tristan asked.

I broke our embrace, flinging back my soaked hair. We stood at the end of a boulevard near an iron gated park. Magnificent brick structures rose to our right, and beyond, the jovial cries and hoots of the revelers all headed towards Fate's palace.

"We head directly into the mouth of the dragon," I said.

I waved my hands and a luxurious gown of twilight hues flowed past Laila's hips. Her wet hair dried, and pinned itself into an elegant style. I did the same spell with Rose, dressing her in purple silk. Tristan and myself I kept smart and simple, enjoying the security of heavy velvet.

"I thought we were going to battle a deity, not go to a party," Rose said, confusion twisting her brow.

"It's not so much party, as drunken orgy," I said. "Inhibition does not exist here. Only the monstrous desires of man set free. We must blend in if we don't want to set off any alarms."

"This will prove to be most edifying," Tristan jested.

"You might think it a joke, but this is a different realm with different rules. You will be surprised how quickly you forget your pride and honor at the flash of an ankle."

I swallowed hard, trying to push away the time I let my own inhibitions slide.

"We stay together following the crowd into the palace. Once there, we must break up."

"You're sure this idea will work?" Laila asked. "I don't like us being separated."

"I'm not sure, but it's our best chance. You and Tristan must get the urn. Blending into the crowd should help conceal you. Us separating is the only way without raising Fate's suspicions. I will go to him, presenting Rose and myself, thus honoring the contract. You both will be released from any further obligation. Well, unless he catches you, of course."

"Just that small snag," Tristan said. Sweat broke out across his forehead once more.

"If we play this right, that won't happen. Fate will be too busy congratulating himself, no doubt rambling on about free will and his grand plan again. This will give you the perfect opportunity to sneak into his study and get the urn."

I flicked my wrist, creating a little golden key attached to a chain.

"This key has the power to open one door, just one, no matter the enchantments. Use it to unlock Fate's study. It's the only way you will be able to get in."

She took it, and slipped the necklace over her head.

"This is all very clever," Laila said. "But one problem remains. How do Tristan and I open the urn?"

I paused.

"That's what I'm relying on you to figure out," I said. "There will be protections. It won't be easy."

She sighed.

"Alright. Let's finish this."

CHAPTER TWELVE

We pressed and shoved our way through the crowd. I hated their silk shoes as they stomped my toes. Floral perfumes and sweat thickened the air, forcing me to hold my breath.

I wanted to blast them all away, however, they presented us perfect cover. We were four souls hidden among hundreds all racing towards the palace.

My blood vibrated with their wants and wishes, their chests glowing with the flames of hidden desires. All selfish and base. Lewd. I didn't know what made me want to retch more. The images of their wanton cravings in my mind, or the stench of claret and armpits on their satin clothes.

"The moment we cross the threshold Fate's eyes will latch on Rose and I. That's when we must break," I said. "It will give you and Tristan a fighting chance to get to the urn."

"What if..." Laila stammered. "What if there is a price?"

A shiver rolled down my spine, and I scratched my chest as if trying to scratch out the sliver of Fate inside me.

"Then it must be paid," I said. "No matter what, you must do what Clotho and Lachesis say. Otherwise this will have all been for nothing."

I took Laila's hand and squeezed, needing her strength. I couldn't shake the feeling I marched to the gallows.

We kept our pace, shoving past a woman from the East, and pushing aside a man in a bejeweled turban.

With every step we neared the palace, the burning in my scar intensified. My breaths deepened, and I tried not to think of the last time I set foot in this wretched place. I had been a fool giving into Fate's temptation. This time, I would not be so weak. So gullible.

My heart thrashed as we entered through the heavy, gilded doors.

The din of the revelers thundered in my ears, echoing through the marble halls and bouncing off pillars. The crowd tightened and pressed against our shoulders.

I curled my fingers into Laila's, wanting to hold on to her a bit longer. To pretend for three heartbeats we were alone, and we were happy. That the horror waiting us did not exist.

I closed my eyes, hating the sensation of letting Laila's fingers slip through my own.

I struggled to breathe as hands, elbows, and arms pushed and prodded my ribs. Gripping Rose, I shoved out of the stream of people, and took a hard right, heading away from Fate's study. Away from Laila and Tristan.

I didn't look back. I couldn't. Everything rested on them now.

I prayed Fate would follow us, leaving his study abandoned.

We kept moving fast in the opposite direction, weaving through halls and courtyards, passing rooms of dancing couples and lavish music, racing across salons covered in silk pillows and dense with hashish.

I wanted as much distance between us and the study as possible.

Come out, come out, Fate. I have your gift.

"What a beautiful creature on your arm. Care to share?" a man asked me. His thick neck glistened with sweat, and his vest buttons threatened to explode.

He reached out for Rose, but I gripped into his fat throat and threw him back. He toppled into a table, splattering wine and macarons over a half naked couple.

Rose's mouth fell open, but I pulled her along.

"You said this place lets the monstrous desires of man run free. Is this truly what humanity wants?" she asked.

I shook my head, having us take a hard left into a billiard room.

Fate, where are you? Show yourself!

"At its core humanity is grotesque. This is why Fate wants to strip us of free will. He feels we do not deserve such a gift. What Fate doesn't understand, is the gift isn't freedom to screw or drink, but freedom to grow. It's about getting the chance to become better, and to overcome our demons."

We ran down a small passage, passing oil paintings of men in ruffled shirts.

Anxiousness started to sink in as Fate remained stubbornly absent. My hand seared hot, and I knew him in the palace. But why was he ignoring me?

Please don't find Laila and Tristan.

Sweat slicked my forehead and I prayed Fate wasn't on to us already.

I turned us down a hallway that stretched into darkness, passing gilded mirrors on either side. The reveler's din faded into silence. Light extinguished. Shadows lengthened.

My palm scalded with pain. Anxiousness turned to panic. My throat went dry and my stomach tightened.

Every second he didn't stand before us, was a second that endangered Laila and Tristan. I couldn't risk letting more time slip by. If we stood a chance, I had to get his attention.

I leaned against Rose's ear.

"No matter what happens, I'm on your side," I whispered.

"Wha—?"

"Fate!" I cried, cutting her off.

Rose pulled back, but I tugged her along.

"What are you doing?" she asked. "You're hurting me."

I didn't want to hurt her, but I couldn't leave anything to chance. It had to look real.

"Where are you, Fate? I've brought my payment."

She fought against me as I pulled her into a dark room of yellow silk wallpaper. A clock on the mantel chimed seven. The blood moon was risen.

"Let me go!"

"Come and claim your prize!" I roared into the emptiness. "Or have you decided you don't want her? I am happy to take her back."

Candles exploded in flame, and fire rolled in the hearth. The door behind me bolted shut, sending my hammering heart into my throat.

Rose squirmed in my grip and tried to kick my knee, but I held her hard against me preventing her attacks.

"That won't be necessary," came Fate's voice. He emerged from the darkness into the firelight, his pointed features sharpened further by the shadows. He tapped the clock face. "Cutting it close. I was worried."

Fear churned in my gut, but I swallowed it down. I hoped he couldn't sense my unease.

"I made a deal with you. I told you I don't break my deals," I said. "I thought you had more faith in me."

He smirked and leaned against the mantel.

"I do. I have great faith in your ability. It's your obedience I question."

I kept my face stone. I would not let him break me.

"Let me go!" Rose stomped her heel in my boot. I further tightened my arms around her waist and wrists.

Fate's eyes latched on hers. She tensed and I hoped she could forgive me. The excitement flaring in his features chilled my blood. He approached Rose, and his mouth parted as if overcome by her.

With a timid touch he cupped her chin. He shivered at the contact, a sickening smile pulling his lips. He stroked her hair, his gaze following the soft waves of her curls.

"It took an age to find you, and another millennia to make you mine. But you are well worth the wait."

She tried to bite his thumb as he traced her lips. I feared his anger, but instead he seemed amused, as if delighted by a playful puppy.

"Let me go, monster," she spat.

"What a spitfire! You don't find many women like this anymore. Truly a lost relic of her time."

She glared at him, standing taller.

"What do you want?" she asked. "My gold? My body?"

He laughed, letting his hands fall too is side.

"Gold is a mortal preoccupation, and I'm not interested in your body, fine as it is. I'm interested in something far more beautiful inside you."

She gasped as he clapped his hand against her chest. I wanted to pull her away from him, but I forced myself to remain still.

"Your spirit, your blood. So perfect. Untouched. That's the kind of soul that will make the thread alive." He pressed harder, his fingers sinking into her skin. She shuddered, and I couldn't take her discomfort anymore.

"She was quite troublesome to fetch," I said, hoping another topic would make him leave her alone.

He ignored me.

"What's this?" He rubbed his hand over her heart. His eyebrows twisted, as if confused. Sickness squeezed my stomach. He sensed something, and I didn't like it.

"Get off me!" she yelled.

"Something warm and unconditional burns in you. Is this...is this love?" His mouth twisted into a crooked smile. "It is! It burns in you, fresh and clean. How disgusting."

"You know women," I said. "Always losing their heads over flutters and flowers."

I hoped he didn't notice the sweat beading on my temples.

First he smirked. Then his eyes darkened and his lips flattened. He turned to me, danger deepening the beautiful lines of his face.

"I warned you not to cross me," he growled.

My throat turned to hot sand, and my blood ice. Hope frayed, and I believed myself falling into an abyss.

He ripped Rose out of my grasp and tossed her to the floor. Her head struck the ground and she moaned. She tried to right herself, but cords appeared binding her wrists and ankles.

I made to go to her side, but Fate opened his scissors and placed the blade against my cheek. I shivered at the sharp bite of the razor's edge eating into my flesh.

He knew.

"You defied me. You broke your promise and went against our bargain. Now, you must be punished."

Menace filled his gaze, and dread pitted my stomach.

"How can I defy you when I brought you what you requested?" I asked. "You have the girl. You have me. What's wrong?"

Rolling his eyes he sighed.

"Don't play stupid. I know Laila and Tristan are both here trying to thwart my little plans. I know you've instigated this mutiny."

A surge of terror, cold and grim, rushed through every inch of my body. My mind raced with what to do. This couldn't be how it ended.

"Yes. It's true," I said, keeping my voice calm. "They are here on a mission to destroy you."

Anger flashed. He pressed his scissors deeper into my flesh. I winced as my skin split.

"You even admit it."

"Of course! How else did you expect me to get the girl here? I had to give them some red herring so they wouldn't suspect me. People don't willingly go into a dragon's den unless their is a uniting goal. Telling them they could win their freedom did the job. Honestly, you're making a big deal out of nothing."

He eyed me. I reached for his arm, and forced his hand and blade down.

"I smell a rat. You're always looking for loopholes."

"You need to be more trusting. Especially of me, when I honored our deal and am here voluntarily before you."

His eyes narrowed.

"Perhaps. Or perhaps I should make you choose who to destroy first." He pulled out the small satchel that contained Laila's soul from his inner pocket. My pulse rushed in my ears. "Do I start by cutting Laila's soul in two? Or would you prefer she watch her son be disemboweled first?

He pulled out her soul, glowing and exposed. One snip and she would be damned forever. I wanted to snatch it from him, but couldn't. I had to stay the course.

I shrugged.

"Have I not made myself clear? I don't care what happens to them. Kill them both at the same time for all I care. Their destinies no longer interest me."

He flicked his wrist, making the thread and satchel disappear, then forced the blade back against my cheek. Steel seared into my wound. It was nothing to the agony knowing he still possessed Laila's core.

"You think me a fool? You planned this little party. You want to win. You want to beat me. But you can't win what you've already lost."

I forced a chuckle. I needed to give him what he wanted most.

My belief.

"Exactly," I said. "You're right. I can't win. In fact, I don't want to."

Confusion riddled his features.

"I doubt that. You're far too stubborn to let go of that mortal emotion nonsense."

"Me? You're the one acting paranoid like common folk. I thought you were a celestial. A god. Above such things."

His right eye twitched.

"These are odd sentiments from you," he said.

"I'm offended you think me incapable of change."

He stared, as if considering my words.

"I don't understand."

"It's very simple. I've discovered you were right all along. About everything."

The rage behind his eyes cooled. Only slightly.

"You cursed me when I showed you the truth you now claim to accept. Fought me. You begged and whined and appealed to my magnanimity. Tell me. What led to such a sudden and drastic change of heart?"

I peered into him, holding his gaze. I hoped he didn't see I spoke only lies.

"As how all changes of heart happen. Experience." I said. "When I left you, I thought humanity was worth saving. Now I return realizing I've been a fool to ever doubt you."

His lips parted, and his cheeks flushed. He cleared his throat, obviously taken by my faith in his nonsense.

"Really?" he asked, the word bright, yet uncertain.

Was he so vain?

"They only ever want and take and betray."

His shoulders relaxed. But he still didn't lower his weapon.

"Yes. It's exhausting and they never learn."

"Exactly, which is why I no longer work for humanity, but against them. Including Laila, and including the boy." The lie was bitter on my tongue, but it had to be said. "My only goal has been to get Rose to you, so we can start the world afresh. Man will become a docile sheep, and we the shepherd."

Rose struggled against her bonds, and her gaze shot daggers into me. Had she not been bound I believed she would have ripped out my heart. I hated making her trust in me waver.

But right now, gaining Fate's trust was more important.

"You bastard!" Rose screamed. "You tricked and damned us all."

"That's what I do, woman," I growled. "I cheat and lie, promising hollow, pretty things to get the results I desire."

Her cheeks flared red with anger and she trembled.

"Tristan trusted you, and you betrayed him. You betrayed both him, and Laila."

I snorted.

"You think I want to bother with that sniveling brat any longer? I've been saddled with him for nineteen years," I said. "As for Laila, that woman deserves no sympathy. She gave up her child to be queen, for God's sake!"

At those words Fate tilted his head, and pressed the blade harder into my skin. Sweat trickled down my back.

"This is where your story crumbles," he hissed. "You would never double-cross that whore. I know you love her."

"I did," I said. "But, as you once told me, why waste my time over a broken woman?"

Silence.

Then laughter.

He nodded, lowering his scissors. I breathed a sigh of relief and rubbed my cheek.

"I'm truly lost for words, Rumpelstiltskin," Fate said. "This is quite the change from last time when you were offering me your very soul for Laila and the boy. I must say, I'm impressed."

"I regret that day," I said. "I was blind, then. Now, I see. Laila played my heart from the beginning. Used me to win crowns and wealth. Tristan will only ever hate me. I've bled for them, I've sacrificed for them, and they repay me with scorn. I'm done hurting. I'm done feeling pain."

Fate reached out and placed his hand on my shoulder. Nausea gripped me as his warmth sunk beneath my clothes into my skin.

"Is that so?" he asked, hope in his voice.

I put my hand on top of his. He shuddered at my touch and seemed to stop breathing.

"I'm sorry I didn't listen before." I wanted to retch at my own words. "Free will is a curse. Ever since I left you I've suffered from its disease. Suffered from the consequence of choice. I was a fool before, spitting on the gift of peace you offered me."

"Don't be so hard on yourself," he whispered.

"I hurt you when I refused the role you offered. I deserve your wrath, but I ask your forgiveness."

Pity overcame his features. He embraced me, holding me against him tenderly.

"My poor child," he said. "I can be merciful, if you are a good boy and do as you're told. And right now, you're being exceptional."

Pulling away, he trailed his thumb down the side of my face. I forced a smile, though my stomach churned.

"I only want an eternity of absolute, unbridled power with a being who always had my best interests at heart."

He smiled, and his eyes glistened with triumph.

"I thought you were a friend," Rose's voice cut in. "I should have let Lord Hochstein kill you. He was right about you, about everything, and I murdered him..."

Those words cut deep.

"Sorry to disappoint."

Fate gripped my upper arms, and squeezed. I'd never seen such joy radiate from him.

"You have no idea how long I've wished for this day," Fate said. "To have someone else finally understand me. To understand the goodness I'm bringing to the world. I've been alone for so long. It's nice to not be alone anymore."

"It just took a little perspective." I looked at Rose, trying to hint to her one last time to trust me still. "*A different point of view.*"

Her brow twisted with confusion, but the anger at me in her eyes cleared. I prayed she understood. I prayed Laila and Tristan would find that damn urn.

"The blood moon is risen. Just a prick and a spell remain, then we can become the family we were meant to be."

Spell?

Fate snapped his fingers. Magic filled the room, and beside the satin chaises appeared that rickety, ancient spinning wheel he'd had me try once before.

The wheel necessary to spin the destiny of man.

Time was up.

LAILA

Tristan and I squeezed between dancing couples, pushing our way to Fate's study.

My heels stuck to puddles of lacquered claret on the polished, parquet floor. Vanilla, cardamom, and the tang of sex filled my every breath. The place made me dizzy with sights, smells, and sounds.

Shoulders shoved into my chest. I pressed them back, and continued onward. We had to get to the other side of the room, to get to the hall where Rumpel said the study was located.

"Get off me," Tristan said to a woman who grabbed his hand, forcing him into a spin. She only giggled.

He pushed her away, only to find himself against a man's chest. Fine silks and lace circled his neck and wrists, but the glazed hunger in his eyes gave me concern.

"Care for some powders?" he held out a delicate silver snuff box.

The man dipped in his thumb and forefinger in the powder, bringing them to his nose and inhaling deeply.

I waved at Tristan to follow me. Now was not the time for politeness.

"No thanks," Tristan said.

Tristan made to walk away, but the man gripped his wrist. He had a lot to learn.

"I won't take no for an answer. Come, you must experience heaven."

"Unhand me, I warn you!" Tristan yelled.

"Let him go," I said.

His lips pulled into a smile, and his gaze fell down to my toes and rose slowly back to meet my own.

"You can come too, my dear lady! You have the most exquisite breasts I wouldn't mind stuffing my face between. What a gorgeous necklace you wear!"

He reached for the key around my neck. Our only way into Fate's study. I prepared to break his nose when...

Thwack!

Tristan ground his fist into the man's jaw. Spittle flung from his mouth as his neck twisted from the blow. He fell back, his head hitting the wooden floor.

Out cold.

Pride filled me.

"God, was he irritating!" Tristan said. "At least he's shut up now."

The music ceased. The couples stopped dancing. They stared.

At us.

My breath stopped.

"You killed Armand!" a woman screeched. Rage and drink filled her pinched face.

We took a step back. She took one closer.

"I didn't," Tristan said. "He's still breathing. You can see his chest rise and fall. He's only unconscious."

She took another step towards us. Others behind her followed.

"I don't think they are in any state of mind to see reason or truth," I said.

"You must pay," a voice came from the crowd.

One more step back. She, one more forward. And another.

"I desire blood tonight, and yours will be spilt," she seethed.

I took Tristan's wrist and we turned and bolted.

Pass through the ballroom, and head towards the hall to the right, Rumpelstiltskin's voice came in my mind. I hoped this was the correct path.

"Get them!" they shouted. "We will not allow Armand's death to go unavenged."

We took a sharp right, shoving our way through another throng of revelers, knocking over candlesticks and tables in our wake. The angry cries of the others lessened the deeper we trudged through the horde. I was grateful to be lost in them.

Peering over their heads arches signaled the end of the room. Slipping past a man fondling a statue, Tristan and I finally spilled out into the hall.

"This place is mad," Tristan gasped, catching his breath.

I wiped sweat from my brow.

"Fate is clever. Those imbeciles are perfect guards. If they don't seduce you, they will kill you."

We kept racing down the hall. The doors stretched out of sight, plentiful and endless.

"Where is this blasted study?" he asked.

"Rumpel said it will be the seventeenth door on the left. It should have a gold sculpted handle," I said.

"They all have gold sculpted handles."

I counted the doors, my lungs burning as we sprinted across the carpets. Time and luck were not on our side.

One, two, three...

"Here!"

A painted door decorated in gold filigrees stood before us. The handle appeared more ornate than the others.

Tristan gripped it, and turned.

"Locked."

Of course.

I trembled as I removed the key from around my neck. Shouts came from down the hall.

They'd found us.

Sinking the key into the keyhole I turned it, a pulse of magic rolling over the door and doorframe.

Click!

"Go!" I said to Tristan.

He scrambled in, I following behind him.

A hand clasped my arm. My heart thrashed in my ears.

"Got you!" the pinched faced woman said. "You will both meet your end."

Tristan wrapped his arms around my waist, pulling me into the room.

"Get off her you crazy bitch!" Tristan screamed.

She clawed into my skirts, tugging me back out into the hall. Others came bounding towards us in the distance.

I couldn't let it end like this.

Swallowing, I pushed all my force and strength into the butt of my hand as I struck her nose. Blood rushed out of her nostrils and over her lips. She released me, and staggered back.

Growling, she made to come at me again.

Tristan pulled me back over the threshold and into the study. He leaned against the door as they pounded their fists against the wood. Forcing my hands steady, I shoved the key in the lock and bolted it shut.

A waterfall of magic fell down again, and I breathed a sigh of relief.

We were safe. For now.

"Are you ok?" Tristan lifted my arms, inspecting for any cuts or bruises.

"Let's get this over with. I don't know how long that magic can hold them back."

I walked towards a set of red silk settees, the fine furniture almost ominous in the dim light. A few candles burned, and the fire was down to its final embers.

Shadows loomed, and I couldn't shake the sensation of *get out*.

"There." Tristan pointed to a large vase beside the fireplace.

My pulse quickened. The malachite urn. The thing that would give us our salvation, or our ruin.

The illustration in my book did not do its beauty justice. Runes were carved into the green stone, which glowed in the remaining fire-light. Elegant piece, appearing heavy and delicate simultaneously.

Tristan rolled up his sleeves and knelt beside it. He felt around and placed his ear against the stone.

"What are you doing?"

"Testing for enchantments."

Impatience filled my veins.

"They're relying on us," I said. "We need to open this. Now."

He reached for the lid. He pulled on the carved nob, only to yelp and throw his hand back.

"We can't do that," he said. "Pater taught me that enchantments are tricky. First, we need time to figure out the right approach. Otherwise we might end up melted."

The clock chimed seven. The blood moon was risen.

We didn't have time.

A lance of fear rushed cold through my veins. The man I loved teetered on the edge of absolute destruction. If we didn't get this damned urn open, I would lose him forever.

Determination filled my heart. It filled my every muscle, surging hot and forceful, eradicating everything in my mind except Rumpelstiltskin.

I clutched a fire iron, and my skin tightened over my knuckles as I squeezed the cold metal. Lifting it overhead, I prepared to bring it down on the vase, shattering it to bits and pieces.

Tristan grabbed my arm, stopping my attack.

"What are you doing?" I screamed. "I need to open it, or else he is lost. They are both lost."

"You can't allow emotions to overtake logic. Not now," he said.

"How can you be so blasé about this?"

"You think I don't care? That it's not eating me inside that Rose is with that *thing* and at its mercy?"

His eyes pleaded for my understanding. My heart started to break.

"I can't lose him, Tristan," I said.

He nodded.

"I know," he said. "Enchantments are riddles, games, and you don't want to break the rules. Pater taught me that, and I think he wouldn't like you shattering our only chance into pieces."

My cheeks flushed hot with embarrassment. I threw the fire iron down, and crossed my arms.

Time kept passing. Precious time.

"Then what do you suggest?" I asked.

He lifted his finger beneath his nose and thought. Kneeling beside the urn again, he inspected the runes.

"I recognize some of these runes." He narrowed his eyes. "I found a book once in Pater's library about such markings. Fascinating things."

I knelt by his side, the rune marks looking like nothing but chicken scratch to me.

"What do they say?"

"I only studied them a little." He chewed his lip and tilted his head. "The urn can be opened."

"How?" I pressed.

He sighed.

"I have to concentrate, Mother." He squinted more, his mouth moving inaudibly. "The urn can be opened by blood. One must prick the finger where the pulse beats, and give an offering to the urn. If found of unselfish heart, the urn will open. If not, the selfish one will die."

I swallowed hot sand and my stomach twisted. Unselfish heart? There had been no one more selfish than I. My abandoning Tristan was proof of that.

"A cruel joke," I whispered. "Clotho and Lachesis placed Rose beneath a sleeping spell with a prick of blood, and Fate requires the same payment for their release."

"Well, best not to think about it," Tristan said.

He took out his dagger, and pressed the tip into his flesh. A drop of blood rose to the surface. Stretching out his arm, he lowered his finger to touch the urn.

I grasped his wrist, and pushed it back to his side. He was right, it was best not to think about it.

"I will give it my blood," I said.

His face twisted with confusion.

"I can't let you do that," he said. "My blood has already saved Rose once before. I would hope it would save her again."

I sighed.

"Hope is not certainty," I said. "I've not had many chances to be a mother to you in your life. To put you first."

"It's not necessa—"

"Now is my chance to right my wrongs." I cut him off. "Let me do this. I won't have you risk your life anymore than you already have."

I held out my hand and motioned for his dagger. He stood silent for two seconds, his lips flattening. Would he relent?

He handed me his dagger.

I stretched out my index finger and placed the tip against my skin. I sliced it in. A shock of pain. A throbbing pulse pounded in my finger, a bead of blood swelling above the wound.

"If this thing kills me, you must find another way," I said. "You must save them."

Tristan met my gaze, red misting his eyes.

"I love you, Mother," he said.

"And I you, Son."

I turned my attention fully on the urn. Its beauty melted into something terrifying. I just had to touch it and Clotho and Lachesis would be freed.

No matter what, you must do what Clotho and Lachesis say, Rumpel's voice came in my mind again.

Somehow I couldn't stop panic from searing my insides. I feared for Rumpelstiltskin and Rose. To be honest, my heart feared more for Rumpelstiltskin.

He wasn't telling me everything, and I hated not knowing.

Stretching out my arm, I extended my cut finger and lowered it to the lid. Shutting my eyes, I pressed my blood against the cold malachite.

Smoldering heat sparked my fingertip. The sensation pulsed into my palm, and traveled up my arm and passed over my shoulder. The burning intensified, and I winced as it wrapped around my heart.

A spear of pain hit my chest. I struggled to breathe as the magic squeezed my heart, compressed my lungs. Fear. Terror.

I believed myself drowning, dying, and I wanted to pull my finger away and break the spell to spare myself.

Stay strong for the man you love. Stay strong for Tristan and Rose.

I pressed my finger harder against the urn, and I felt myself scream although I heard nothing but the rush of blood in my ears.

Darkness.

Relief.

A voice called me in the distance. I stirred. The voice called again, muffled.

Something patted my cheek.

"Mother!"

My eyes flashed open. Tristan knelt beside me, worry etching the lines of his face.

"Am I dead?"

He shook his head, his lips pulling into a smile.

"No, you're not dead."

The world stilled around me as I came back to. He slipped his arm behind my back, and helped lift me to my feet.

"I thought I'd lost you," he said.

"I'm ok," I said, facing the urn. "I hope it was enough."

The lid remained sealed. Dismay started to sink in my chest.

The floor vibrated beneath my feet. A crystal glass trembled on the mantel, rocking towards the edge until it fell and exploded across the parquet.

The entire room quaked.

Tristan and I held each other as the urn toppled on its side. The lid flung off, skittering across the rugs.

Mist flooded out of the vase, and a chill nipped at my skin. The gray haze swirled and twisted as it rose off the ground. The cloud split. Shapes formed.

Human shapes.

I blinked, not believing my own eyes.

Two women stood before us, lurid togas wrapping their bodies that resembled hard marble. Their eyes glittered with ancient secrets, while the soft curves of their lips and cheeks spoke of youth.

They looked at each other. The woman on the right touched the one on the left's arm, while the one of the left touched the other's shoulder. Smiles stretched across their faces as they embraced, tears streaming down their faces.

"To look on your face again!" Her voice sounded like honey.

"We're free. Finally free," the other replied.

They separated and wiped their eyes with their togas. I dared a step towards them.

Their gazes fell on me, with their ethereal and mysterious eyes. My breath caught in my throat. I stood in the presence of deities.

"Clotho?" I asked. "Lachesis?"

The woman on the left came to me and grasped my hands.

"Yes, my sister Lachesis and I thank you. You rescued us."

"We'd lost hope of ever being released," Lachesis said.

"How did you figure out how to open the urn?" Clotho asked.

The clock chimed a quarter after. My heart thrashed and acid burned the base of my throat.

"I'm afraid there's no time for all that," I said. "We need your help to stop your sister, otherwise all is lost."

Their faces twisted with confusion.

"Atropos?"

"Today is the Blood Moon of Phlegethon," Tristan said. "Atropos is about to end free will. Only you can help us stop him...I mean, her. You did it once before."

Lachesis chuckled.

"While I can't wait to break her neck, your worry is unfounded. We made sure she can never fulfill her foolish and reckless dream. We've ensured the protection of the world."

Irritation burned in my gut. I thought these would be the last two I would have to convince about Fate's powers.

"You mean ensuring protection by placing a princess beneath a sleeping spell? The Princess Rose?" I asked.

Clotho's eyes narrowed. Lachesis raised an eyebrow.

"How do you kno—"

"I woke her," Tristan blurted.

Their skin paled, and Lachesis staggered back.

"What do you mean 'woke her'? It's impossible. Only a..."

"Only a prince can wake her?" he asked. "Only the son of a king, and of a woman who overcame an impossible task, can break the spell? I'm the product of such a union. I'm the way Fate was able to finally take Rose."

Horror filled their eyes, and Clotho even trembled. Fury blazed in Lachesis' face, and she clenched her jaw. She stood before Tristan, barely an inch between them. Tristan remained firm and tall.

"How could you do this?" she hissed. "This is detrimental. You ruined everything we did. Every sacrifice we made. Everything is now rendered useless."

"Fate, I mean, Atropos, swore to kill me otherwise. To kill my mother and my father. I didn't have much choice."

She crossed her arms shaking her head, and turned away from him. She paced. Clotho clenched her hands into fists, and red blossomed over her chest and cheeks.

"There's always a choice, and you chose to damn everyone," Clotho said.

"Once she starts the spell, there will be no way to stop it. It's finished," Lachesis added. "Foolish mortals!"

I couldn't take it anymore.

"Enough!" I yelled. "We are wasting time pointing fingers. We are all to blame, and now we need to stop Fate before it's too late. You must have some idea? You must know some weakness?"

They stopped, looked at each other, and nodded.

"Her scissors," Lachesis breathed. "Her scissors are the only way to end her. Her power is linked to them. To her entire being. It's how she will perform the spell."

The hairs on the back of my neck raised.

"What spell?" I asked.

Clotho bit her lip.

"Atropos will cut the palms of her new Spinner and Measurer. Each will be given a part of herself, a sliver of immortality and magic. It's how she will get three members, of all one blood. A new family to replace us."

Horror spread through me thinking of the scar Fate already made on Rumpelstiltskin's palm. Of how a piece of Fate already lived within him, linking them together.

"What if one already has their palm cut?" I asked. "What happens to them when Fate is destroyed?"

Their lips flattened, and their eyes fell to the floor. My stomach churned and my heart fell to my feet.

I understood what Rumpelstiltskin didn't want me to know.

CHAPTER THIRTEEN

Slub:

Noun: A soft thick uneven section in yarn or thread

Verb: To draw out and twist (slivers of wool, cotton, etc.) slightly

RUMPELSTILTSKIN

"**S**it here, princess." Fate dug into Rose's shoulders, forcing her beside the spinning wheel. "Do smile. That frown does nothing for you."

Flicking his wrist, a copper, square sectioned measuring rod appeared. Power radiated from the gleaming metal, making me shiver.

Fate balanced it between his palms, smiling as he ran his gaze the length of the copper. He held it before Rose.

"Do you know what this is?" he asked.

She shook her head.

"This is how the lives of men are measured. You see, Rumpelstiltskin over there will spin the thread we need. Pure souls, unwritten and blank. With this measuring rod, you will take that twisted fiber of life and decide if they receive a life that stretches centuries, or one that doesn't last a breath."

Rose paled. I hated the glee in Fate's voice.

"You mean, I decide when they will die?" she asked. "I can't do something so horrid."

"Of course you can't, because that's my job." Fate pulled out his scissors, and my stomach lurched. "Once you determine the length that pleases you, only then do I deliver the final cut where that life ends."

A clear ring of metal filled the space around us as he opened them, followed by the clap and chop as he closed the blades, snapping the air. His smile made his beautiful face ugly.

Putting his scissors away, he held the rod out to Rose.

"I grant you your new scepter, princess."

Her lips flattened, and her eyes filled with hate.

"I don't want it," she said.

Fate flexed his jaw, but forced his muscles to relax. He tilted his head, cracking his neck.

"Just a little stage fright is all. Once you feel it, once its power flows in your veins, you'll change your mind."

Taking her hand, he forced the copper rod in her palm. He wrapped her fingers around the metal, until she gripped it tight.

As he released her, she flung the rod over the silk settee. Striking the parquet, the metal clattered and rolled to a stop.

Rage stiffened his face and lit his eyes. He wound his fingers in her hair, and tugged forcing her to face him. She cried out, trying to pull free.

My heart pounded, and fear gripped my throat. While I was grateful for Rose's disquiet, for any precious time her refusals bought us, I couldn't risk his anger harming her.

I needed to find another way to delay his plans, without raising his suspicion.

"Stupid girl!" Fate screamed. "You dare disrespect such a celestial and sacred tool?"

I ran my hand down the spinning wheel, giving it a good whirr. The clacking broke his attention from her, letting it fall on me instead.

Bending down, I picked up the rod. The magic within truly was deep and consuming. Arousing, even. For a heartbeat, I wanted its power.

I handed it out to him.

"Let's not lose our temper," I said. "She's not yet at the under-standing we've reached. Maybe give her a bit more time to come around."

He eyed me, then took the rod from me.

"We don't have time for that, lest we miss the blood moon and have to wait another millennia."

Pity, that.

"I know, but she must be willing." I touched his shoulder, feigning care.

For the first time, worry etched the lines of his face, and he rubbed his mouth with his hand, as if thinking what step to take next. Inwardly, I rejoiced. Hope started to bubble.

He sighed, and turned back to Rose.

"Unfortunately, Rumpelstiltskin speaks the truth. I can't force you to take the measuring rod, but you should know the facts about your foolish choice to decline."

Rose furrowed her brow.

"Are you threatening me?" she asked. "I don't care if I die."

He nodded, slowly, pursing his lips.

"I know you don't," he whispered. "But you care for Tristan. You care for your father, and your kingdom. You want to save them, well, this is how you will do it." He knelt before her, taking her hands and softly rubbing them with his thumbs. "If not, if you decide to be self-ish, I will kill that boy who has stolen your heart. I will destroy your kingdom and your father once and for all. But, as I said, the choice is yours."

He held the measuring rod back out to her.

Fury blazed in her face, and she cursed him beneath her breath as she snatched the rod away.

"For Tristan's safety, for my father's and my kingdom's, I will take it."

He stood, joy dancing in his features.

"Beautiful! You look just like Lachesis all those millennia ago!" He stroked her cheek, but she turned away. He frowned, letting his hand fall to his side. "You're drowning in guilt. I sense it rising from your skin. Self doubt, anxiety, panic... You fear you are harming the world in accepting this role. But you are saving it, and isn't saving the world what you always wanted? To be a hero?"

"Not like this," she said.

He shook his head.

"We are saviors, Rose. We will bring relief not only to your kingdom, but to all peoples." He pointed at me, and sweat wet my back. "Rumpelstiltskin thought like you. He challenged me at every step, but eventually he saw the beauty in my plan. He believes, as will you."

Her cheeks reddened, and her knuckles turned white clenching the rod.

"I will never believe."

"We shall see." He pulled out his scissors again, the silver flashing in the firelight. "Give me your hand. Come on, we haven't much longer left."

A lance of panic pierced my core, and my blood froze. Dammit, where were Laila and Tristan?

"What are you going to do to me?" she asked.

"Give you the same scar as Rumpelstiltskin. It's the only way for the magic to work. As soon as I cut your flesh and impart my powers, we will be bonded by blood. We will be family, and family always believes in each other."

He grabbed her hand, the shears blazing between white and shadow.

My throat turned desert, and my heart thundered, burning in my chest. A few heartbeats more and it would all be over. I never knew sickness could grip me as it did. My options were run out.

Still, I wouldn't let him damn her like he did me.

"Don't be afraid," he cooed. "This is your rebirth! We will weave the souls of men. Stop squirming!"

My mind reeled with what to do.

I needed any seconds I could squeeze out of him. Anything to give Laila and Tristan the tiniest sliver more of time to open the urn. If they were even able to open it...

He brought the blade down to her palm, the point digging into her flesh.

Blood rushed in my head, allowing for little else but panic and determination.

"Brace yourself, this won't be pleasant," he told her.

I touched Fate's shoulder, and squeezed. His muscles tensed beneath my touch, and he leaned slightly, ever so slightly, into my palm.

A flame ignited within his soul. A flicker of desperation...for me.

I swallowed hard.

"It's beautiful to watch the transformation you did to me from this vantage point. With a clear head, and heart," I said.

I hoped Laila and Tristan would hurry.

He cleared his throat, and his flame burned brighter. Hotter.

"Yes. I still recall the sensation when I imparted myself in you. We became one that day."

I hated him, but I couldn't let him know. I touched his cheek, skating my finger over his dips and angles. He closed his eyes and breathed deeply, as if wanting to inhale my scent.

"I can't stop thinking of the other time we became one. The night we shared."

He looked at me, narrowing his gaze.

"I thought that memory disgusted you."

If only he knew. I still felt him on my skin. I wanted to scrub him away until nothing remained, but it would never be enough to erase him completely. I lost a part of myself that day.

But I couldn't think on that now.

"It did," I said. "But not anymore. No other ever gave me such pleasure, and I want to reach that sensation, that abandon, again."

Surprise etched his face, and heat flushed his skin. My heart thundered, praying he'd believe my lie. His flame exploded in his chest, longing for me, desiring more of my honied words.

He put his scissors back in their holder at his left hip.

I kept my relief hidden inside. I needed a few more seconds.

Fate took my hand, and lifted it to his eyes. He traced my scar, his touch gentle, loving. I hated every inch of me he grazed.

"It still looks just as the day I made it," he said. "I waited centuries to find one like you."

"And now you have me. Forever."

His soul raged in an inferno of lust and desire. I forced down my disgust.

I pulled him towards me, until our chests pressed hard together.

His heart pounded against my skin. He caressed the side of my face, disbelief and wonder dancing behind his darkening eyes.

He wet his lips. I braced myself.

"An eternity of this awaits us," he said. "But for now, you must be patient. I must first finish with Rose."

He released my hand. He turned, setting his sight back on her.

No.

Digging into his shoulders, I spun him back around and kissed him. He fell into my embrace, moaning softly as I deepened our kiss. He ran his hand up my spine, coiling his fingers in my hair. His tongue rolled hot in my mouth, and I gripped his head, demanding more of him.

I only had one shot.

Our mouths moved in a fast rhythm, and his desire throbbed against my leg. I cascaded my hand over the hard ridges of his chest, down to his waist. Down to the buckle of his trousers.

"This is the passion I've been craving from you," he gasped as I attacked his neck.

"There's more to come."

I pushed him against a wall, digging my thumb in his jaw. His eyes lit with fire. I locked his mouth with mine again, taking away his breath. Making sure he couldn't see what I did next.

I slipped my fingers an inch into his trousers. He whimpered wanting me to go lower. Running along his belt, I made for his hips. Towards his scissors.

They were they key to this spell. If he didn't have them, he couldn't harm her.

I pressed myself against his desire, hoping to fog his mind into oblivion. I grazed the cold silver of those blasted blades.

Slipping my other hand into his trousers, I stroked him, trying not to retch. He moaned deeply into my mouth.

Victory washed over me as I curled my fingers into the handle of the scissors. I tugged on them, trying to free them from his holster. They remained stuck.

Dread shot ice through my veins

His hand shot up to my throat, clawing into my neck. I scratched at his hands, trying to pry him off me. Pain shot down to my shoulders, and I gasped for air as he crushed.

Screaming curses, he blew me back. My head struck the floor, white and black dots spotting my vision. I coughed and choked, rubbing my neck. Rose rushed to my side, trying to help me.

"You prick!" he seethed. Passion still swelled his lips. "How dare you trick me."

I forced myself to stand, putting her behind me. Lividness filled Fate's eyes.

"Hurts doesn't it?" I asked.

"You've taken me for a fool. Played me since the beginning. Pulled the wool over my eyes."

I laughed, though it burned.

"Did you actually think I could ever want you? That I would ever believe in you?"

Pain befell his gaze, as if I wounded him deeply, but anger took it back over.

"We could have experienced heaven together."

"I don't want your heaven."

He bared his teeth and flicked his wrist. Invisible bonds wound tight around my wrists and ankles, rendering me useless. I hated his magic was still stronger than my own.

"I warned you not to cross me. Now you will stay tamed and trained beneath my boot forever."

He turned his sight back to Rose who still remained behind me. Blood rushed in my ears and panic set in. He waved his hand, and Rose glided towards him.

I fought against my veiled chains, the ropes cutting into my flesh. They only strengthened, cutting deeper. I had to get to Rose. I had to stop him.

I wanted to cry out to Laila and Tristan, to scream to tell them to hurry.

Rose kicked Fate's knee, and tore at his face. He growled, gripping her arm and forcing her back in the chair.

"Remember, if you want Tristan unharmed, if you want to save the world, you will do as I say." She stopped struggling and he pulled out his scissors. "You will both believe in me. I swear you both will see once it's done."

He pressed the blade to her palm again. My heart thrashed and I only heard the pounding of my own blood. I cried out as I tugged at my bonds, the magic like razors severing my skin.

Could I free myself? No, I knew I couldn't. Hope dwindled to ash in my core, but I wouldn't stop until he cut her palm.

"Rumpel!" Laila's voice cut through my panic. Hope again gushed within my chest.

Fate's hand and the scissors clapped to his side, as if by force. My heart sang seeing Rose's palm uninjured.

Magic released me, and I fell to the ground. Pressing into the stone, I righted myself and faced Laila, Tristan, and two other women. Clotho and Lachesis. They appeared as four angels, and relief flooded me.

However, the red misting Laila's eyes gave me pause. She knew something.

Fate stepped back, holding out his scissors as a weapon. His right eye twitched, and a wild, crazed look stiffened his features. Behind that brewed fear.

"How they hell did you get out?" He demanded. "How is this possible?"

They shook their heads, sadness and pity painting their expressions. One stepped forward, putting out her hand to Fate. He swallowed, and his mouth twisted with disgust.

"Look what you've allowed your rage to do to yourself," she said. "You wear the guise of a man now. Where has my sister gone? Where is Atropos?"

"She died the day you both betrayed me," he spat. "I couldn't even look in the mirror and see you both in my reflection, in me. I took this new form, erasing every part of you."

The woman let her hand fall back to her side.

"We are sorry we hurt you," the other said. "But what you wanted was wrong. Detrimental. You drove us to the brink. You left us no other recourse."

"So you crippled me? Silenced me? You stole my full powers, stole who I was. You clipped my wings, showing no mercy like I was never your sister at all."

"And did you show us mercy when you imprisoned us in an urn? I think we are even," she said.

Fate chuckled darkly.

"I doubt that, Clotho."

"We implore you now to stop while there's still time. You will destroy the world in trying to save it," Lachesis said.

Fate's eyes narrowed.

"I will only destroy what ought never to have existed in the first place," he replied.

Clotho let her gaze fall to her feet, and sighed.

"Still blind after all this time?" she asked.

He shook his head, clenching his jaw. His right eye twitched again, as if he was unraveling.

"No, I see clearly. More clearly than any of you. I have a vision. I am bringing peace to the earth, something the both of you never had the guts to do. You prefer to let humanity suffer. Free will is a disease, and it ends tonight."

Lachesis grabbed Fate's hands, and stared into his eyes. Fate stiffened, and I thought he would pull away, but he didn't.

"Free will allows hope. If you end free will, you are destroying hope. You will cause them to suffer greater than ever."

"But they won't suffer from the burden of choice anymore," he whispered.

"There is still time to turn away from this madness," Clotho added.

"You always think you can talk me out of everything. You never have faith in me. You never listen. You only lie and deceive."

Clotho reached out and touched his arm. He shivered, and his face tightened and contorted with confusion.

"We are listening," she said. "But what we hear are not the words of logic or reason, but of pain. We're sorry for the pain we caused you. We're sorry if you think we didn't have faith in you. We do, we just want to help protect you from yourself."

A tear slid down his cheek, and he started to tremble.

"Stop trying to fill my head with words. Useless words."

"Please, turn away from this poisonous dream," Lachesis said.

"Give us the scissors, and we can be a family again."

Fate whitened, horror and anger etching the lines of his brow and mouth. He pulled away from them, and stepped back. He rubbed his face, then wiped at wherever they had touched him. As if trying to get rid of their residue.

"Lies," he spat. "We can never be a family again, because we never were. Family doesn't betray its own blood. That's why I'm making a new family. A new world order. There will be no betrayal. There will only be destiny. Beauty. A perfect symmetry that this universe needs."

Clotho and Lachesis neared Fate again. He stepped back.

"Atropos, give us the scissors. This is your last chance. We don't want harm to come to you, but we will have no choice. We are the protectors of free will, and we are bound to defend it. Don't let it end like this. Don't force our hand."

Mirth curled his lips into a smile. I didn't like the triumph in his eyes.

"That's where you're out of luck. Only one can end me, neither of them you," he said.

They nodded, then looked at me. My veins iced, and an invisible hand squeezed my insides.

"It must be you," they said.

"Me?" I asked.

Fate laughed, the room quaking with his amusement.

"See, Rumpelstiltskin? See how wicked they truly are? You don't know what they are asking of you."

"What do you mean?"

He chuckled again, staring at his sisters. At the two women I had hoped would save us.

"Shall I tell him, or would you prefer to elaborate on this lovely little detail?"

My pulse quickened, and my breaths burned as fear tightened my chest. Terror. I glanced at Laila. Her eyes remained red, and they told me everything.

Still, I couldn't accept this was it.

"Tell me," I roared.

He shrugged.

"It's quite simple," he said. "If I die, you die."

My heart plummeted into the depths of my being. Everything I ever feared, ever dreaded, came alive in that sentence. For two seconds, I wanted to run, to cry, to beg.

But there was no use. This was the hand given to me, and I had to play it.

"Explain," I said.

He smiled, a wicked, vile smile I wished I could rip off his face.

"Those Pythin sisters knew what you'd become. They saw the shadow lurking within you, in your future. They saw me there. Then, when you offered me your barren, beautiful palm, well, it allowed me to seal the deal. In imparting my magic, I linked us by blood and soul. I tethered you to me, as I will do with Rose. This is how the spell works. We must be three, but also one. Family."

"Laila was right," I whispered, though I could no longer feel my own lips. Maybe I didn't even speak at all. "You were the key the Oracle said was within me."

He smirked.

"Guilty," he said. "Now you can watch the new age be rung in. Rose will be our sister, and we will be inseparable."

Growling, he lunged at Rose. She scrambled away, toppling over her chair. But he was faster. Grasping her arm, he held the razor edge of his scissors against her skin.

"You will not touch her!" Tristan screamed, charging Fate.

He tackled him at his waist, knocking Fate back. His scissors flung out of his grip and clattered across the stone floor. Fate cursed, clutching Tristan by the neck.

Laila rushed to Rose, pulling her back and away to safety. Tristan kicked and squirmed, until Fate flew him against a wall.

A blast of white magic shot at Fate. He blocked it. Another of blue, this one from Clotho. He blocked again, shooting back his own of green.

A wildness overtook him I'd never seen before. This was preservation. Desperation.

Danger.

Orbs of light and color shot past me as they battled. As I walked towards Fate. As I walked without thought, except one.

The scissors lay at my feet. Unattended.

Red light whizzed past my ear, but I didn't care. It was nothing to the cold sweat running down my back, or the lump in my throat as I tried to swallow down my dread.

A crack of purple lightning grazed my right shoulder. It didn't faze me.

Only the glint of the silver held my attention. Bending down, I gripped the cold metal, shivering at the sensation. At what they meant.

The explosions and flashes of magic stopped. Fate turned to me, his eyes wide as I held his weapon.

I rushed at him, locking his head in the crook of my arm. I pointed the blade into his neck, as he had done to me so many times.

Then, he laughed. The bastard laughed. It took everything in me not to cut out his voice right then and there.

"You won't do it," he said. "I know you too well. You would never give up your powers. Your life. The girl..."

He struggled, but I pressed the razor deeper into his muscle. He hissed, and his blood trickled warm over my knuckles.

I loved the thrill of it. It helped numb me from my own fear.

"You don't know me at all," I said in his ear. "If you did, you would be terrified right now."

He swallowed. For the first time sweat dropped down his temples.

"Stop this. There's no point. You're only wasting time. We are missing the blood moon!"

"Shut up!" I yelled. "Don't test me."

"Come now, you won't do it. You have too much to lose."

"Give me Laila's soul," I hissed.

"Always with that woman!"

I tightened my grip, and cut further into his neck. He cried out and winced. Panting, he dug into his pockets, pulling out the little, velvet satchel. He handed it to me, and I motioned with my head for Laila to take it.

She trembled as she ripped it away. Opening it, she pulled out the glowing, golden thread Fate had ripped out of her.

"Let it fall back into your chest," I told her.

She stared at me, gratefulness and distress bleeding from her eyes. "Rumpel..."

"Do it quickly," I cut her off. I didn't know what I would do if she tried to give me her sympathy. I couldn't break. Not now.

She nodded, lifting the thread over her heart. Closing her eyes, she lowered the string, her soul slipping beneath her skin and back into her core. As the final inch sunk into her, her eyes flashed open and she sucked in a breath.

The vibration of her life force hit me, pulsing and alive. I knew all was well.

"Now what?" Fate growled. "Are we to remain locked like this for eternity? Or will you let me go? You won't end us now she's made whole. You won't give her up. You never have."

He was right. I had never given her up. I never could.

I looked into Laila's gaze. Tears streamed down her flushed cheeks. We both knew.

"I told you I'd return your soul to you," I said to her. "Everything I've done, I've done for you and Tristan. I love you."

I turned my eyes away. I couldn't take the sorrow swelling her face. Fate squirmed, causing himself to choke in my hold.

"How about a new deal?" He gasped, almost begged. I loved his nervousness. "I might own you, but I can allow her to stay with you. Remain by my side, and we can leave all this mess behind."

"The mess you caused," I said.

"The mess you chose."

I smirked. I drew a deep breath.

"I did choose," I said. "I did choose the darkness. I did choose to fight against love. But now, I choose to do what's right. I'm done making deals."

Tranquility overcame me. An odd and eerie peace. As if for the first time, I accepted my destiny.

I buried his scissors deep into his chest, and twisted. Shock overcame his expression, followed by anguish. Then grief. Pain.

The steel scraped against his bone and sinew, piercing his heart. Blood and gore gushed out of him, warm and slippery over my hand.

My veins exploded in fire, and I heard someone scream.

I screamed.

I twisted the blade again, sinking it deeper. Pain, strong and unfor-giving, lanced my heart. Fate gargled words to me, his mouth filling with blood. Hot copper filled my own mouth.

Everything in me begged me to stop. A voice inside my mind tempted me with summer days. With loving embraces as I took Laila in a meadow.

My fingers slipped on the handle as I turned it again. I grunted as fresh agony doused my body. Scalded my skin.

The scissors were severing me. Breaking me. My bones, my soul. I trembled to my core. My legs gave way, Fate and I falling to the cold stone.

Fate screamed as I pulled out the scissors only to plunge them in him again, sinking them into his core.

My hand gave way. Strength left me. Laila and Tristan rushed to my side, and pulled me away.

Fate clawed after my foot, reaching for anything. Crimson surrounded him, and his skin held no color.

"We could have done it," he rasped.

His flesh burst into flame. He shrieked for a second or two, until his cries evaporated with his lungs.

Then, he was no more.

My hands shook and my teeth chattered. The spark and fire within me flickered, then extinguished. The magic that kept me living drained from my body, only my dying flesh left in its wake.

I was so cold. I hated the coldness.

Laila trembled as she patted my chest and my neck, searching for a wound she could tend. Tristan fell to his knees, and held my hand.

I didn't want to die.

I didn't.

"You can't go," Laila wept. "Not like this. Not after everything."

Her words swirled together, but I loved the lilting sound of her voice. Like a lullaby. I wanted to brush her cheek, but I couldn't lift my arm.

"This is as it must be."

"No, I won't allow it."

"Let me go."

She lifted my hand to her lips and kissed it.

"But I love you," she said.

Her tears fell hot on my skin, mingling with my own. If only she knew the love I held for her. My devotion to her.

"I tasted salvation on your lips once. I owe you all I am."

"I will be lost without you," she moaned.

I wished I could kiss her. I wanted to taste her one last time.

"You will always have me in your memories."

I turned to Tristan. Red glazed his eyes.

"Pater?"

"Go in my...pocket. The...the ring is there. Take it, and...give it to Rose."

Words burned my throat now. Burned my lungs and my bones.

Wiping away a tear, Tristan did as I asked. Pulling out Laila's ring, he gripped it tight.

"Thank you, Pater," he said. "For everything."

"I would do it all again...to know you are safe..."

Every breath tore through me.

Laila stroked my cheek. I wished I could have felt it. I felt nothing.

"There will only ever be you," she said.

I don't want to die

"I love you," I whispered. "Evermore."

The world blackened around the edges. She and Tristan both warped and dissolved into shadows.

I don't want to die

Blackness.

Nothingness.

Cold.

LAILA

My world disintegrated into ash. Everything I was ended with his last breath.

He couldn't leave me like this.

Not like this.

"Come back to me!" I gripped his shoulders and shook him. He was asleep, that's all. If I could just wake him. "Come back!"

I pounded my fists against his chest, trying to reach his heart. Trying to force it to beat again.

He remained still. Asleep.

Gone.

Emotion burst out of me as tears ran down my face. I collapsed on top of him, squeezing his limp body in my embrace.

"Please come back."

Tristan touched my arm. Rose sat by my side. She wiped away her own tears.

"I'm sorry," he whispered. "He was a good man. He sacrificed everything for us."

My hands shook as I cradled Rumpelstiltskin's head between them. Bending down, I kissed his lips.

They were ice.

"We must give him a blanket," I said. "Something to warm him. He's frigid."

"Laila..." Rose said.

I stroked his hair. And I wept. Bitterly.

Why weren't they bringing me a blanket?

"Don't just stand there, help me warm him!"

Tristan lifted me away, turning me into his shoulder.

"He's gone, Mother," he said.

Lies.

No.

Truth.

Horrible, wicked truth.

"I hate this." My voice was rough. "To have him, only to lose him again."

"You will get through this," he said. "We all must get through this."

Could I get through this?

Clotho and Lachesis stood before the remnants of Fate's corpse, then bent down retrieving the scissors from the ground. Blood slid down the steel and off the tip.

I wanted to bury my face in Tristan's shoulder, but I couldn't stop watching them as they approached Rumpelstiltskin's body. One on either side of him, they knelt, their gowns pooling around their legs.

They stared at each other, then nodded. Lachesis sunk her fingers into his chest.

Rage overtook my grief tensing my muscles. I tore out of Tristan's arms, curling my fingers into fists. I wouldn't let them mutilate him.

Lachesis tugged, pulling out a thread from his depths. It appeared the same as the thread of my own soul, except his didn't glow like mine. The fibers were gray.

Dead.

I shivered.

"What are you doing?" I asked. "Leave him alone."

"There must always be three," they answered in unison.

My heart raced as they wrapped his thread, his very soul and being, around the scissor blades.

"You can't mean," I whispered. "No. I won't allow this."

"It's not up to you to decide. The scissors must have a new owner."

Clotho chanted over his body, her mouth moving in odd ways speaking words I didn't understand.

"Stop!" I shrieked. "He didn't want this."

"But he will live."

I admit I loved the thought. I felt his kiss on my lips. I smelled cedar and woodsmoke on his skin. I heard him tell me he loved me.

I wanted him back, but steel and blade would forever bind him.

"Not at this cost," I said, hating the words as they left my tongue.

Their smiles straightened, almost frowned.

"There is no other choice. It must be done, or else the universe will be unbalanced. Dangerous. There must always be three."

They placed the scissors atop his chest. The thread sparked and sputtered. Pale light trickled down until the entire string glowed bright in gold. Just as the golden thread I once watched speed through his fingers all those years ago.

The string, his soul, fused into the silver metal of the scissors. Light doused him, and his skin pulsed with radiant spirit and vibrancy.

He sucked in a breath, and his eyes shot open. He clasped the scissors tight, as if he instinctively knew they were his very essence now.

A tear rolled down my face. I wasn't sure if it came from elation or resentment.

He looked down at his chest, down at his feet. He found Clotho and Lachesis. I hated the confusion in his features.

"I thought I was dead," he said.

I wanted to weep hearing his voice again.

"You were," Clotho said.

"But we need a third. We need a spinner."

"You are now a defender of free will, like us."

He sat up, and stared off into nothing. A mixture of emotion danced behind the gray of his eyes, brewing in the storms he always held. The storms I fell in love with.

His eyes found mine. We said everything to each other in that glance.

"What of my own freedom?" he asked them.

They smiled, as if his fear was foolish.

"We know this isn't what you wanted, but it is your destiny," Lachesis added. "As it's always been since the beginning."

Rising, he stood tall and strong. He didn't tremble anymore. He didn't wince with pain. He was perfect. Whole.

Walking to me, he took my hands in his. They were warm now, flowing with life.

I smiled, holding back the bitter joy coursing through me. We embraced, and I fell into him, fell into the ecstasy of having him back though I hated the cost.

He cupped my cheeks, wiping away my tears with his thumbs. Utter rapture sparkled in his gaze, and his usual wry smile made my knees weak. God, I loved this man.

"Is it worth it?" I asked as we gripped our hands tight together, holding them between us. "You've become what you feared."

He leaned his forehead against my own. I shivered as his hot breath rolled down my nose and chin.

"It's worth any price to be with the woman I love."

EXCERPT FROM "THE CROWN: A DARK RETELLING OF THE TWELVE DANCING PRINCESSES"

A young man stood on a scaffold waiting for death. Guns and drums surrounded him. A priest read proverbs from a Bible, the spine cracked with age.

"Prince Englebrook, by proclamation of King Rupert, you have been condemned to death on this day, the sixth of May in the year of our Lord 1791. May God have mercy on your soul," a man announced to the crowd. He reeked of palace protocol.

The prince remained standing tall, not a quiver daring betray the fear bleeding through his eyes. Three guards made to remove his coat, but he put out his hand stopping them. With a shake of his shoulders he slid his coat off himself. His fingers twisted within his cravat, unraveling the jungle of fabric from around his neck. He unbuttoned his shirt revealing his chest and peeled the collar away from his skin.

One of the guards grabbed his hair, yanking his head back causing him to stumble. Still he did not protest. Scissors gleamed in the sun as they ate through his tresses, leaving jagged tufts of hair in its wake. The guard threw his severed hair to the crowd, and a dozen hands rose into the air hoping to catch a souvenir.

It made my stomach turn.

"I never thought I'd see the day a prince be executed. Now I've seen twenty-seven!" an old woman said next to me. "Still they come, all wanting a taste of the power the king offers. Greed is what I call it."

Wire-like gray hair sprung out from beneath her moth eaten bonnet. What teeth remained in her mouth were a mixture of black and yellow. Her eyes shone with an odd mixture of childlike simplicity and severe reality.

"I think that harsh," I replied. "They are only doing what comes natural to the truly desperate."

"Truly stupid is more like it," she retorted. "Is power ever worth risking one's own life?"

"That depends on the reward," I said, pulling on the strap of my satchel.

I had not come for a chat. Leaning on my cane, I stepped away from her and neared the scaffold.

The prince put out his hands and they were quickly tied behind his back. Head held high, the guards escorted him to the railing. The jeers of the crowd died away in anticipation of his final royal address.

"I die having failed King Rupert. I die having failed your kingdom," he said, voice remaining firm. "I accept my judgement. I am no coward. I only pray another will be stronger than I and fulfill his majesty's quest."

"Pull the lever already!" course men chanted between swigs of whiskey.

Four guards latched onto the prince's arms and tugged him back towards the guillotine. They pushed him down onto his stomach and locked stained wooden boards around his neck. The blade hung ready to plummet towards the feast of soft flesh below.

The crowd was in a frenzy, and a roar filled the square. They clapped their hands around their mouths and hooted and hollered to the executioner. They hungered for blood.

"Get on with it!" a woman holding a small child jeered.

A loud cry cut through the growl and drums began to rumble. The priest's prayers disappeared behind the tumbling succession of sticks against taught leather. The prince closed his eyes.

I had seen a hundred men do the same in war. Even the bravest could not face their death square on. For this, he had my pity.

"Pull it!" the crowd snarled.

A click and a rush rang out followed by splitting bone.

It was done.

Cheers erupted.

Blood rained down the wood and pooled in the crevices of the cobblestones. Elbows jabbed into stomachs as onlookers scurried towards the scaffold, white handkerchiefs in hand. They dabbled up whatever crimson they could as grim tokens and mementos. A prince's blood could fetch a pence or two, enough for a loaf of bread to slake their hunger.

Disgust filled me not at the death of a youth, but at what the king had made of his own people. Animals living in squalor. That would all change soon. I dove my hand into my satchel, grounding myself within the silken layers of the cloak that promised me the crown.

The prim man who had read the charges reached into the basket for their newest trophy. His fingers coiled within the prince's blonde hair as he held the head to the crowd. The eyes that minutes before showed fear were now vacant, the lips slack and skin flushed blue.

"King Rupert requires a new challenger," he said. "One who is cunning enough to solve the mystery baffling his majesty. Any man may accept this quest as long as they are resolute. As a reward, they will inherit King Rupert's throne. But," he held up the prince's head even higher, "if the contender is unable to solve the mystery in three days, he will face the same fate as our freshly departed Prince Englebrook."

I cleared my throat to rid the dry prickle that seized it and pulled again on the strap of my satchel. The reassuring heaviness vanquished the trepidation he tried to instill. This was the moment I traveled so far for, and I would not abandon my fellow citizens as had our king.

"I will be your new challenger," I called out.

An ocean of eyes locked on me. Several onlookers crossed their chests that were stained with dirt and muck.

I approached the scaffold, planting my cane firmly into the cobblestones. Pain split through my ankle with each step, but I ignored it as always.

"Tosser!" Someone yelled out.

The man's face pinched into a sharp point and his eyes flashed with

irritated doubt. It was a look I was all too familiar with. It was a look I
was wearisome of seeing.

"It is illegal to mock the crown," he warned.

Guards brought him the basket and he swiftly dropped Prince
Englebrook's head inside as if it were nothing more than a banana peel.

"I do not mock," I replied standing right below him. "I want to be
his majesty's next challenger."

Laughter bubbled out of the throats of the crowd causing my every
muscle to bristle.

"Sir, you are quite lame," he said, pointing at my cane.

"I am well aware," I shot back. "Does that exclude me?"

He blinked several times as if thinking what to reply.

"No, I suppose it doesn't," he said.

He wiped the smattering of blood on his hand away with his
kerchief and flew down the creaking stairs.

"I'm Sir Charles Langley," he said, holding out his hand. "And
you are?"

My lip curled in revulsion seeing red still smeared across his signet
ring.

"Ross Daltry," I replied.

Awkwardness filled the space between us as I continued to let his
arm hover. He stretched it further towards me until he saw I would
not be swayed. I had little use for etiquette anymore.

"Mr. Daltry, if you are quite determined..."

"I am," I said, growing impatient. "Is there a document I sign? Or
do I make a pledge? I wish to be in his majesty's services immediately."

The man seemed dumbfounded for a second or two, as if thinking
my mind would still change. He could never guess the determination
rushing through my every vein.

"A meeting with the king is usually all that is required, Mr. Daltry. I
will inform his majesty of your intentions to become his –" he paused
at the word, "–champion."

"Is that all?" I inquired further.

He sighed.

"Arrive this evening at the palace gates. State your name to the
guards. Everything will follow suit from there," he said. Then, he hesi-

tated. "I...suggest you take these remaining hours and think through what you are doing. I do not want the king's time wasted on a rash moment of bravery. Men half your age and...vigor...have met the blade."

I glared at him wanting to put him beneath the blade.

"I do not waste time," I said. "Not my own, and especially not the king's."

Find *The Crown* at a wide selection of online retailers!

THANK YOU!

I sincerely hope you enjoyed reading this book as much as I enjoyed writing it. If you did, I would greatly appreciate a short review on Amazon or your favorite book website, such as Goodreads! Reviews are crucial for any author, and even just a line or two can make a huge difference.

ALSO BY GENEVIEVE RAAS

NOVELS

The *Spindlewind Trilogy*, a dark fantasy, paranormal romance retelling of Rumpelstiltskin

Spin

Twist

Break

༺❀༻

NOVELLAS

Crimp

A gothic romance. Enjoy as a stand alone work, or as a companion to the Spindlewind Trilogy

The Crown

A dark retelling of the Twelve Dancing Princesses

ACKNOWLEDGMENTS

There are so many people I want to thank for supporting me while I wrote this book.

First, I have to thank the amazing Hannah Stahlhut. You've been there every step of the way, and I don't know where this trilogy would be without you. Through the ups and downs, you've helped guide me through.

My husband, Rafi, you also gave me an amazing amount of support! Thank you for putting up with me talking about these characters the past years.

To my parents. Thank you for always believing in me! Your love and encouragement has been more helpful than you can imagine.

To all my other family, friends, and YOU, the reader, THANK YOU!

ABOUT THE AUTHOR

Genevieve Raas is an international bestselling author living in the US with her husband and rather haughty Chihuahua, Mr. Darcy. When she isn't writing dark fairytales or fantasy, you can find her plotting out her next travel destination.

A graduate from Indiana University, Genevieve holds a Master's Degree in English and a Master's Certificate in Professional Editing. She has worked as Lead Transcriber on several published anthologies, including: The Collected Stories of Ray Bradbury, Volume 2 and the New Ray Bradbury Review.

Now, she is venturing out on her own, into the wilds of untamed lands and untold stories.

You can connect with Genevieve on her website, or by simply clicking the social media links below!

genevieveraas.com

facebook.com/genevieveraas

amazon.com/author/genevieveraas

twitter.com/genevieveraas

goodreads.com/GenevieveRaas

bookbub.com/authors/genevieve-raas